CROWD PLEASER

AUTISM: THE EFFECT ON THE PARENT

Also by the author

Early Bird, a short film produced by Julian Grant.

CROWD PLEASER

AUTISM: THE EFFECT ON THE PARENT

BY VERONICA GILLOTTI

Order this book online at www.trafford.com
or email orders@trafford.com

Most Trafford titles are also available at major online book retailers.

Printed in Victoria, BC, Canada.

ISBN: 978-1-4269-2049-3

Library of Congress Control Number: 2009939383

Our mission is to efficiently provide the world's finest, most comprehensive book publishing service, enabling every author to experience success. To find out how to publish your book, your way, and have it available worldwide, visit us online at www.trafford.com

Trafford rev. 11/03/2009

www.trafford.com

North America & international
toll-free: 1 888 232 4444 (USA & Canada)
phone: 250 383 6864 • fax: 812 355 4082

In Memory of Mr. Thomas P. Hogan

About the author

VERONICA GILLOTTI, WHO IS employed as a legal secretary, resides in New York City with her son and dog. Like her son, she enjoys pizza, bike riding around the city, and shopping at GameStop.

Synopsis

FAITH INITIALLY THOUGHT THAT her son, Hunter, was deaf, because, by the age of two years, he'd not uttered a peep. Her dearest friend and confidant, Frank, advised her to seek professional help.

During the summer, Faith painstakingly met professionals to collect documentation for Hunter's diagnosis.

Fired from her administrative position, Faith haphazardly found temporary employment as a carpenter's assistant, a dog walker, and she even held the title of landlord.

The evaluation from professionals concluded that Hunter was in the autistic spectrum.

Overwhelmed by the diagnosis, angered by the dog walker, and distressed by her roommate, Faith searched for Hunter's biological father. Unfortunately, he was in a supervised time-out.

It ends well: Frank was enthusiastic about Hunter's enrollment in a special needs school. Faith was employed as an administrative assistant. The roommate returned with a job offer Faith couldn't refuse.

Contents

Evening Chat

FAITH BALANCED HER WINE and baby monitor in her hands and bumped the door open with her butt. She situated herself on the top step of her stoop, sipped her wine, and placed the monitor beside her.

Faith sniffed, made a "what's that smell?" face, then kicked the banana peel off the stoop thinking, "People are pigs."

A squeak of the door. Faith smiled, watched a tall, sassy, blond, feminine male exit his building. He high kicked, fashion strutted over, and joined her on the stoop. "Nice walk, Frank. Do you practice in your apartment?"

Frank did another high kick. "I don't need to practice, it comes *au naturel.* You, my dear, should practice the walk, and wear something sexy to help me help you get a man."

Faith peered over her mug and smiled at Frank. "We wear the same size—ten." She sipped her wine.

Frank retorted, "How dare you! I'm a size eight. Don't stare at me with those green eyes, with that 'I love this wine' face, missy." Frank gently reached for the mug. Faith grabbed the mug defensively, placing it beside the monitor. "Don't touch my drink!" Frank sniffed Faith's personal space. Faith lashed out, "Stop. That's aggravating!"

Hands on hips, Frank replied, "How much of that have you had today?"

Faith laughed. "First today. I won't drink in front of Hunter." Frank responded, "I would be drunk 24/7 if I were his parent with all that screaming!"

Faith fired back, "I'm working on quieting the screams."

Frank spotted a man further up the street, pointed. "Now there's a nice man for you?"

Faith followed Frank's gaze. "That carpenter loading the truck?"

Frank surmised, "Faith, he obviously has a job, he could buy you dinner."

Faith sipped from her mug. "That guy would suggest I cook dinner before he went out to cheat."

Frank hung his head. "How many years have I been trying to find a man for you?"

"Oh, a good number of years, but who's counting."

Frank rubbed his long legs. "I need a tan, summer starts tomorrow. I can't wait to lie in the park."

Faith, in a trance, did not respond.

Frank repeated, "I can't wait to lie in the park! Faith, don't bring that kid anywhere near where I lie in the park."

Faith put her cup down. "I'm sorry, what did you say!"

Frank was stern. "That kid is driving you nuts. If I had to deal with a kid that screamed all day, I'd be drinking more than wine."

Faith answered somberly, "I love my little caveman. I hope Lila can handle him. I've got to get to work on time."

Frank agreed, "Yes you do, and so do I tomorrow." He crossed his legs. "Who's Lila?"

Faith sighed. "She's Sam's wife."

Frank glared at Faith. "Who's Sam?"

Faith cleared her throat. "Sam, the guy in the deli, has a wife, Lila." Frank slid closer to Faith, "Hope she shows up on time and wants to keep the job, not like the others."

Faith responded, "At least the first day anyway. We're in for a long summer if I have to keep finding new sitters."

Frank slunk down the stairs, struck a pose. As a dog walker passed with several hounds, he stage whispered, "Hello, hello young man?" Frank spoke his thought, "Doesn't that dog walker remind you of someone?"

The dog walker ran with the dogs and turned the corner, moving out of sight. Faith laughed, sipped wine. "He sort of physically resembles the father."

Frank glared. "He could be the father."

Faith laughed. "He ran by fast—he was on to you."

Frank slipped beside Faith. "He likes animals, you like animals. It would be perfect."

Faith sipped her wine. Frank seductively added, "He had fine broad shoulders, a muscular build. If you closed your eyes, you wouldn't know the difference."

Faith slurred, "You speak as if you were in love."

Frank laughed. "Get the words out clearly. Face it, you let a another man slip away."

Faith stared out into the street. "Men leave."

Frank retuned to the top step and fluffed her hair. "You need a good thinning, too much hair."

Faith snapped, "You need to relax. How many years have I been telling you that?"

Frank whispered, "huh," stepped gracefully down the stairs, posed. Faith yawned and smiled. "Frank, we'll look for a man tomorrow night."

"I'm going for a walk, I don't know what I'm going to do with you."

Faith laughed. "I remember the father, he was hot."

Frank shouted, "Hot, huh—cute, he was cute all right. He disappeared, poof! Gone."

Faith finished the wine. "Time for another." Frank rolled his eyes. The monitor roared. Faith grabbed mug and monitor. "Got to go."

Frank threw his arms in the air. "Hurry before that kid starts to scream." Faith turned her key, pushed open the door, ran into the building. Frank shouted, "I'll call you."

Lila meets Hunter

HUNTER CENTERED HIS BUTT on the skateboard and flapped his hands by his sides. Faith gently shoved the skateboard with her foot. Crossing the kitchen floor, the board rolled to a stop between the table and the bathtub. Hunter squealed with delight and waited for another push. Faith knelt down before Hunter. "Hey little man, look at me. Turn yourself around, look." Faith made directed eye contact with Hunter, but he turned his head away, grabbed her foot, and placed it on the board. Faith shoved the board back across the room to the bookcase. Hunter again laughed delightfully.

Hearing a bang on the door and buzz of the doorbell, Faith peeked out the peep hole. "Oh shit." She inhaled deeply and opened the door to a woman of about five foot five with wrinkled skin, her hair pulled back in a ponytail, her body wrapped tight in a faded green bathrobe; she wore faded pink slippers. Faith cheerfully greeted the woman, "Hi."

The neighbor snarled, "I hear rolling and screaming, I'm trying to sleep!"

Faith smiled politely responded, "We'll keep it down."

Faith closed the door. Hunter rolled over to the television, hopped on the basketball, bounced off, rolled on the floor, and stopped in front of the refrigerator. Faith hid the skateboard in the tub and joined Hunter at the refrigerator, which was decorated with pictures of Hunter and homemade transformer magnets. Hunter pointed aggressively at the refrigerator. Faith ignored the visual demand, continuing to apply her makeup by the mirror. Hunter growled. Faith answered, "Yes?" Hunter bent his arm at the elbow, stomped, and forcefully flung his arm at the refrigerator. Faith hugged Hunter, then held him eye level. Hunter turned his face away. She put him down. "You have to say the words, 'I want, I want.'"

As Faith opened the refrigerator and retrieved the juice bottle, Hunter switched on all the stove burners. "Oh my God!" Faith spun them off and knelt down in front of Hunter. "That would be a *no*!"

Hunter turned away, grabbed the powdered cleanser from the window sill, and flipped it over. Powder poured out. Hunter rocked and flapped his hands. Faith passed Hunter the juice and grabbed the cleanser out of his hands. Hunter peacefully sat in his foam chair in front of the television with juice. Faith opened the cabinet under the sink, pulled out a paper-towel roll, ripped off a few panels, placed the towel roll on the floor, and began to clean. Hunter grabbed the towel roll and ran to the bedroom. Faith demanded, "Hunter, bring it back," as she continued to clean up the mess. She peeked into the bedroom. Hunter jumped high on the bed, then landed, efficiently, with his back on the paper-towel roll.

Faith huffed in frustration. She returned to the mirror and applied mascara to her lashes. The door buzz shrieked. Faith stabbed herself in the eye. "Shit." She wiped her eye, swung open the apartment door, and shouted down the dimly lit stairwell, "Hello." She stepped back into the apartment and managed to bang her head on the wall and slam her knee into the tub. She limped into the hall, checked her knee, and listened for the tap of footsteps. "Hello, we are on the fourth floor."

A faint "Okay" twirled up the stairwell. Lila arrived at the door short of breath, entered, and sighed heavily. "So sorry I am late, Miss. This is for you, from my husband." Lila handed Faith a bag.

"For me? That's nice, thanks." Faith opened the bag. Inside was a foil ball with coffee. "Is that a bagel and coffee?"

Lila spoke softly and smiled. "Yes, Miss. From Sam. He's glad I have a job now."

Faith yanked a chair from under the table for Lila. "Please sit down."

She removed the coffee from the bag, opened the lid, took a sip, "Woo, very hot, I'll save it for work."

Lila nodded. "Okay miss, where's Hunter?"

Faith peeked into the room. "He's watching his cartoons." Faith placed the coffee back in the bag on the kitchen table. "Come meet him, but he may not acknowledge you." She held up the skateboard, "Hunter likes to sit on this but you have to push it." Faith placed the skateboard, soccer ball, and basketball in the tub.

Lila covered her yelp with her hand over her mouth. "I did not see! Your tub is in the kitchen!"

Faith laughed, "Yes the tub's in the kitchen, these apartments are old. Feel free to give Hunter a bath if he should climb in—that is what he wants. Hunter doesn't talk yet although he is a big two-year-old."

Lila observed, "You keep your spices on the window sill. I do the same at my house. Is the air conditioner on?"

Faith hurried to the window and showed Lila the controls of the air conditioner. "Sure. Just tap this button, on, you can adjust the temperature."

Lila examined the buttons and peeked over at the stove. "You cook, Miss?"

Faith smiled, "Not if I can help it."

Lila gasped, "What, does Hunter eat?"

Faith opened the refrigerator and removed the box of chicken nuggets and the pizza box—his menu. "Heat up either one for three minutes in the microwave." Faith returned the boxes to the fridge. "Okay, Lila, let's meet Hunter."

Faith began to re-roll the paper towels that covered the futon. Lila smiled, touched Hunter's head gently, and observed the mural of baby jungle animals on the wall, awestruck. Faith posed like a showroom model, "Lila, this is my bedroom and living room."

"The painting is beautiful, Miss." Lila sat beside Hunter, who immediately plopped down in her lap.

Faith smiled. "He must like you. Lila, I can fold the futon into a chair for you." Lila gave Hunter a kiss on his cheek. Hunter pushed her away, focused on the cartoon. "Lila, unfortunately, he does that a lot."

"It's okay, Miss." Lila reached over for a book and opened it in her lap. Hunter flipped the book closed and placed it back on the shelf.

Lila laughed. Faith stood. "Lila, there is one more room, where you can watch you own programs." Lila followed as Faith described, "This is Hunter's room, where he sleeps."

Lila pointed to the mural of transformers, amazed. "Did you do that, Miss?"

"Yes, I don't think Hunter likes transformers yet, but I do. Aren't they manly?" Lila laughed. "Lila, Hunter rules the roost. Should he take over this television you can move to one in the next room." "Okay, Miss. I need your number at work please. "

Two giant steps brought them back into the kitchen. Lila swung the chair away from the table and sat. Faith found a pencil among the cluttered on the table and wrote her number. She pressed down too hard on the pencil and it cracked. Lila dug in her bag and handed Faith a pen. Faith wrote big so there would be no confusion, then handed the paper to Lila.

"I'll call when I get to work."

"Okay, Miss. We will go at lunch over to where my husband works?"

Faith smiled, "Sure. Hunter likes that spinning display at the deli. I have the number there if you're not home. Have fun."

Faith checked the clock. It was 9:10 AM. "Wow! It's late! Lila, I have to move fast. He drinks lots of juice, please water it down. I have to go."

Lila stood next to Hunter, who was fixed in front of the TV. Faith grabbed her bag from the kitchen table along with the food bag and dashed out into the hall.

Lila called after her, "Miss, Hunter is a beautiful child."

Faith swung back and bear hugged Hunter but he shoved her away. She winked at Lila. "Have a good day."

Lila followed Faith to the door, watching as she exited. Faith heard the door bolt click closed, paused, checked her bag for her work identification, muttered, "I hope this works," and trotted down the stairs.

The Warning

THE ELEVATOR DOORS SLID apart, displaying a white marble reception area with a magnificent view of New York's East Side. Faith signed in 9:30 AM at the reception desk although the clock read 9:50 AM.

Mr. Harold, an oversized man who signed the checks for the firm, entered. "Faith, I saw you running down the avenue."

Faith smiled. "You did? Where were you?"

"On the air-conditioned bus. I should run with you, I might lose a bit of this." Mr. Harold maneuvered his stomach to one side of himself.

Faith responded, "Mr. Harold, start out slow." Mr. Harold smiled and proceeded past reception area to his office.

A young woman, wearing a blue suit that matched her eyes and carrying a mass of waved hair, tapped Faith on the shoulder and said, "Wait one minute."

Joan, Faith's office mate, entered the fish bowl conference room and stole some muffins from the catered breakfast. Faith smirked and dropped the pen on the receptionist desk. Joan handed her a muffin and they walked down the hall together. "Thanks, Joan. Now I have coffee, muffin, and a bagel with cream cheese."

Joan laughed, "Breakfast and lunch. How's your son, Faith?"

Faith exhaled noisily. "Not talking yet. I'm so concerned."

Guy pushed his squeaky mail cart past Faith and Joan. Faith commented, "Guy, I hope none of that is for my boss. Your cart represents too much work."

"This run is for the thirteenth floor."

Joan touched Faith's arm. "Kids talk when they are ready, Faith." Guy pushed the cart further into the office. As Faith plopped down at her computer and clicked it on, the phone rang. She glanced at the caller identification number. "Let that roll into voicemail."

Joan agreed, "Good idea," as she lifted open the lid of her coffee and flipped through the newspaper to the horoscope section.

Faith's cluttered desk held folders piled high, scattered papers, several pen boxes, and clips. She cleared an area for breakfast. The telephone rang again. Faith peeked at the extension, grabbed the receiver, and said, "Good morning, Mary. Sure I'll be right there." Faith slapped the phone on the receiver, sighed, and placed her coffee near the computer screen, the muffin beside the keyboard, and the cream cheese bagel back in the bag. Faith rose, rolled her chair under the desk, and sighed.

Joan watched Faith. "When you get back, we'll read the horoscopes."

Faith voiced concern, "If I get back."

Faith walked down the hall to Mary's office, she paused at the door to inhale and exhale deeply. She knocked, opened the door, and entered. The sunlight from the window blinded her, but Mary's shadowy arm waved for her to sit in the guest chair. Mary finished her conversation on the telephone with her back to Faith. Mary wore her exquisite navy blue suit; her hair was tightly pulled into a bun and her nails were manicured blood red. Faith waited nervously, skimmed the snapshots taped to the wall of office picnics and holiday gatherings, all showing the staff with big smiles.

Mary hung up the telephone abruptly. Faith spotted a stain in the middle of her white top and threads hanging like fringe from her slacks.

Mary began, "Faith, I have reviewed your file." Mary folded her hands over the closed folder. Faith sighed and straightened herself in the chair. Mary leaned forward, "Faith, you have been late every day this month. Not good."

Faith leaned forward on the chair in an effort to look attentive. "Every day? By how much?"

Mary's voice rose, "That's not the point. We expect you here at 9:15 AM to be ready to work at 9:30 AM. You do understand."

Faith smiled, "Yes, I understand. Sometimes my sitter's late, which results in my lateness."

Mary stared, "Can anyone help you in the morning?"

"I'll make sure I arrive on time."

Mary clearly stated, "This is your last warning. We, the firm, cannot make any exceptions on enforcing that rule. Please make an effort."

Faith stood up to leave and answered, "9:15 AM it is. Thank you Mary."

Mary immediately picked up the telephone receiver and pounded digits with a vengeance. Faith walked to the door, then turned back toward Mary, "Do you want this shut?"

Mary snapped, "Yes." Faith closed the door softly and walked down to hall to her desk.

Mom's Hearing Test

HUNTER HUNG ON THE navy blue sheet draped over the window gate. Faith tossed a paper-towel roll on the bed. He released his grip on the curtain, landed with his back on the paper-towel roll, and flung the roll out like a fishing line. Towels floated down to the floor. Hunter gently walked on the path.

Faith lay on the floor behind Hunter. He was enthralled with his animated DVD, which had the volume off. Faith tapped on the toy drum, paused, banged on the coffee table, paused—she got no response from Hunter. He flapped his hands continuously, along with the movements on the screen, and added a side-to-side rocking.

"Hunter, Hunter! Can you hear this Hunter? Hunter! Hunter! Oh Hunter, how about this lyric?" Faith played a keyboard attached to a book, "Hunter. Hunter!! Look, Hunter."

Hunter did not respond, but he tore apart the paper-towel squares, still focused on the animation. Faith stole the remote and raised the volume. Hunter covered his ears, screamed, and turned the volume down on the television. "Don't you know what you're doing, little man?" Faith tapped on the drums again, then shook the tambourine. No response.

Faith leaned back on the futon. Hunter rocked from left to right and waved his hands. The doorbell shrieked. Faith jolted to attention, but

Hunter had no reaction. "Hunter, can you get the door? We have a visitor! Hunter, Hunter, help me get the door." Faith knelt beside Hunter and held him very close. She gave him a big kiss. Hunter elbowed her away and remained focused on the television, his small butt balanced on the shrunken paper-towel roll.

Faith passed through the clutter of toys in the kitchen, adjusted the shower curtain over the bathtub, reached for the buzzer, pushed the door button, unlocked the door and opened it an inch, then returned to the living room. "Hunter, good boy, look at Mommy. Hello, I love you, good boy."

Frank entered and observed Faith banging on the drum and shaking the tambourine behind Hunter's head. He asked, "What the hell are you doing?"

"I'm testing Hunter's hearing."

"He hears fine. Look at him, he watches that DVD. He rocks to the music."

"Frank, the volume is off. Why won't he answer me?"

Frank rolled his eyes and swung Hunter high into his arms, "Faith, take him to the doctor. Get him checked out. He should be saying a few words like, 'Mama is crazy,' 'juice' and the word 'no.'"

"We have an appointment at a neurologist tomorrow."

Frank plunked down next to Faith. "About time, bitch."

Hunter activated rewind on the DVD player. Faith clapped her hands behind his head. Hunter swung around, took both her hands in his, and placed them on the drums. He returned to his post in front of the television.

Frank laughed, "He told you, didn't he? Stop the torture. Go to the store while I'm here. I've got to get home before my visitor arrives."

Faith stood up quickly, "Ten minutes is all I need." She ran into the kitchen. "Where's my bag?"

Frank swiped the throw from the futon and tossed it up in the air over Hunter. The blanket landed on Hunter's head. Hunter pulled the blanket off his head and let it fall to the ground. Frank shouted, "Faith, it's hot in here. Is the air on?"

She moved toys around, searching for her bag, "The air is on, I'll turn it up higher." Faith went to the window and cranked up the conditioner.

"How's the new sitter?"

Faith flipped the newspaper from the kitchen table to the floor and tipped the chair. "She is great. Hmmm."

Frank stood in the doorway between the kitchen and Hunter's room. "Get going, bitch."

Faith returned to the bedroom. "Could you hand me my bag please?"

"Where is it?"

"Under your foot."

Frank handed Faith the bag. "Hurry!"

Faith closed the door of the apartment, wiped beads of sweat from her forehead, sat on the stairs, checked for the wallet, sighed, and ran downstairs.

The Neurologist

FAITH HELD HUNTER'S HAND and hailed a cab. One swerved into the corner and stopped. Hunter dropped to the ground and, with his arms and legs sprawled out on the sidewalk and his face turned toward the sky, he kicked and screamed.

As Faith knelt to comfort Hunter, her bag dropped just above his head. "Yikes, sorry baby." Faith reached over to pick him up. He kicked, screamed, and pulled Faith's hair. The cab took off. Faith distracted Hunter with kisses and reclaimed her hair from his clenched fist. Hunter kicked more, narrowly missing Faith's nose. She dug in her bag for a squeeze toy and held it close enough for Hunter to see. He kicked the toy out of her hand. Faith searched her bag for another distraction. She felt the small hairs on her neck rise, her face grow hot and her cheeks flush as the screams grew louder. "Hunter, let's count, one, two, three."

Passers-by tossed out intrusive hints, "Miss, he's hungry. That's a hungry cry."

"The kid needs sleep."

"She has a tummy ache. Poor girl."

A young woman ran to Faith with her cell phone in hand, ready to dial. "Why is he lying on the ground? Shall I call for help?"

Faith felt her face flush. "We are fine, he is okay, keep moving."

Hunter's screech continued. Angry people with mean expressions crossed the street to escape the high-pitched wail.

Faith found the bubble bottle in her bag, opened it, and blew bubbles. The bubbles floated over Hunter's face, calming him eventually, and the scream subsided. He rose to his feet, swiped at—then caught—some bubbles. Faith took his hand as she continued to manufacture bubbles. "I hope we make it four blocks."

At the neurologist's office, where they stopped, Hunter dropped to the ground with an ear-piercing scream and kicked like a wild animal. Faith gulped and felt her face flush again as a crowd gathered. Faith yanked Hunter to his feet and wrestled him through the door. His yelp jolted the receptionist to her feet. Hunter clutched the door molding.

The receptionist rushed to assist. "What can I do to help?"

Faith directed, "Can you grab his feet please?" The receptionist held Hunter's feet, Faith held his legs, and they backed into the office together and gently laid Hunter on the floor.

His screams had escalated to an animal type screech. Faith spoke over the noise. "Hi, we have an appointment with Dr. West in ten minutes."

The receptionist yelled back, "Your name please?"

"Faith Parker."

An oversized clock that hung above the reception area caught Hunter's attention and hushed the wails. The receptionist checked the schedule, gathered some forms from the shelf, attached them to a clipboard, and passed the clipboard to Faith with instruction, "Please fill out these forms and return them to me."

"Sure." Faith rolled her eyes, and, with one hand, she held Hunter by her side while she searched through her bag for a pen. The receptionist handed Faith a pen. She wrote her name. As she released her grip on Hunter, he impulsively bolted for the door. "Oh hell." Faith dropped the pen on the floor and the clipboard on the desk. She scooted after Hunter, caught hold of his shoulder, and pulled him back. Hunter landed on his butt with a deafening scream.

Above the yowl, the receptionist yelled, "Good catch, Ms. Parker."

"He keeps me on my toes." Hunter cried and climbed into Faith's arms. He proceeded to stab his chin in her chest. "Ouch, Hunter, that hurts!"

The receptionist ordered, "Please follow me into the waiting room where you will be able to close the door."

Faith nodded appreciation, "Great, thanks."

Faith held Hunter lovingly in her arms and kissed his face. He rubbed his tears on her shirt. They entered the waiting room and plopped down on the couch. Hunter climbed into the toy box and attempted to close the lid. Faith prevented the closure with a book from the bookshelf. She sat near the toy box on the couch. Above, a neon flash screen slowly scrolled the words *Keep the Doctor's Office Clean.* The sign had Hunter's attention. Watching it, he rocked while Faith finished the forms. Another mother entered with her child, and they both stared at Hunter.

Faith said defensively, "In his previous life, he worked on Wall Street."

The woman gave Faith strange look. The receptionist entered the wait area and said, "Ms. Parker, Hunter, this way please."

Faith, Hunter, and the receptionist entered the doctor's office.

Dr. West reached from behind his desk to shake Faith's hand. Hunter beelined directly to the toy box in corner of this office.

"Hello, Dr. West."

"Please sit down, Ms. Parker."

Faith took a seat in the guest chair.

Dr. West sat, adjusted his legal pad, clicked the only pen on the desk a few times, and tested the ink with long scribbled lines on the paper.

Faith laced her fingers together and held Hunter in her lap. "This is Hunter. Say 'hi,' Hunter."

Hunter wiggled out of her grasp and went over to the toy box, where he lined up some blocks.

Dr. West smiled. "He'll be okay there. I have a few questions regarding the pregnancy, etc."

Faith nervously fidgeted in the chair, "Go ahead."

Dr. West proceeded with the question, "Was it a full-term pregnancy?"

"Yes, full term, no problems, that is correct."

Dr. West scribbled down the answer. Hunter brought over a toy, placed it in Faith's lap, and darted back to the toy box. The doctor asked, "Were there any problems at during the delivery?"

A quick response from Faith, "No, no problems."

Dr. West scratched his eyebrow. "Does Hunter have a brother or a sister?"

"No. Hunter is the one and only."

Dr. West cleared his throat, "Is the father involved with Hunter?" Faith replied, "No."

Faith reached for Hunter. Dr. West scribbled on his pad. Hunter came over with a toy top and placed her hand on the top. Faith slid to the floor.

Dr. West asked, "Does he always do that when he wants something?"

Faith turned her attention from Hunter back to Dr. West. "Yes." Faith pushed the top handle down, making the top spin. Hunter flapped his hands. Faith commented, "Look, the top spins, Hunter."

As Faith placed her hands back in her lap, Dr. West peered over his glasses. "Faith, the flapping of his hands that he does is called stimming."

Faith repeated, "Stimming, an actual term."

Dr. West continued, "Will he try to spin the top?"

Hunter placed Faith's hand back on the toy. Faith directed, "Hunter, you try."

Hunter placed Faith's hand on the top again. Faith answered, "No. He has to get used to things before he tries them on his own. He would need a few hours with this top." Faith remained on the floor and spun the top with Hunter.

Dr. West continued, "Did Hunter cry a lot as an infant?"

Faith returned to the chair. "No, he was a very good baby."

Dr. West clicked his pen a few times, then asked, "Any ear infections?"

From the toy box, Hunter took each animal and placed them in a straight line on the floor. He stopped and admired his work, and he stimmed. Faith responded, "Hunter had many bad ear infections, plus I had to change his baby formula twice. You can see Hunter moves well physically, but he does not speak."

Dr. West watched Hunter stim for a few moments. Faith reached for Hunter's hands and held them still. "Why does he move, stim, his hands like that?"

Dr. West jotted down notes and replied, "Self-stimulation."

Faith kissed Hunter's cheek. "He also puts items in the store I have placed in my cart back on the shelf. I can't take him shopping. He covers his ears if noise is overwhelming, and he watches cartoons with the sound off."

Hunter bolted toward Dr. West's computer and slammed his hand on the keyboard. Dr. West quickly reached over to guide Hunter away from the computer. Hunter wriggled behind his bookcase and maneuvered his way back to the computer. Dr. West rolled his chair back. Hunter, annoyed, marched to the exit and hung on the doorknob. Unable to open the door, he let out a scream and raised his pitch.

Dr. West spoke over the scream, "Is this common?"

Faith shouted, "Yes, when he wants to go and can't move out quickly enough, he screams. Are there any other questions?"

Dr. West shook his head and replied, "No, Faith."

Faith sighed, "What should I do?"

Faith hugged Hunter tight in her arms and kissed Hunter's cheek. Hunter rammed his chin into Faith's chest. She released her grip. As he wriggled to the floor, his screams persisted.

Dr. West remained behind his desk, at attention, and delivered his sentence in a controlled manner. "Hunter falls in the spectrum of autism, which is very broad. My immediate suggestion—connect Hunter with a speech therapist who will evaluate him and work with him. Here are a few therapists that I have worked with."

Faith took the list that Dr. West handed her, folded it, and placed the folded paper in her pants pocket. She scooped Hunter up in her arms and balanced him on her hip. Dr. West moved from behind his desk, held the door open, and continued, "The second step—get him tested by an audiologist, a speech therapist, an occupational therapist, and the Board of Education. There are a number of good schools in the area that specialize in teaching children like Hunter."

Hunter wiggled out of Faith's arms and stood quietly near the exit. Faith gripped Hunter's hand. Dr. West guided Faith down the hall.

Faith asked, "When can I expect your report?"

Dr. West said, "I'll walk you out."

Faith swooped Hunter up in her arms.

Dr. West cleared his throat. "In a couple of weeks, you'll receive my report by mail. Bring Hunter back in a few months. You can call any time if you have any questions."

Faith shook hands with Dr. West. "Thank you again, Dr. West."

Hunter opened door to the street. Faith ran close behind. Dr. West observed from the doorway. Faith waved and swung Hunter into her arms. "Hunter's heavy."

Faith looked back at Dr. West, and he nodded. Faith lowered Hunter down to walk, and she held firmly onto his hand as they zigzagged toward home.

Escorted Out

Faith swung the apartment door wide open and sprinted back into the bedroom. Hunter stimmed in front of the television. She leaped onto the futon, tugged the curtain down, opened the window gate, and leaned out. Hunter crawled under Faith, stepped out on the fire escape, and screamed with joy. Faith smiled, "Hunter, you can't go out there. Mommy needs to look for Lila." Faith searched the street below. No Lila. Faith pulled Hunter in from the fire escape. The door buzzer shrieked. Faith check the clock; the time was 9:10 AM. Faith commented, "About time."

Faith rushed into the kitchen, checked the clock radio: 9:15 AM. "Oh man! Which is correct?" Faith jerked on her sneakers, adjusted her slacks, and buttoned her oversized blouse. Lila entered the kitchen out of breath, pulled a chair out, sat down, and said, "So, sorry, Faith. Sam could not find parking, I had to help him look."

Faith glanced at the clock. "It's okay, Lila. I have to run. I'll call when I get to work." Faith lunged out the door.

Lila went to the door. "Wait, Faith, I have breakfast for you." Lila handed a paper bag with coffee to Faith.

"Thanks, Thank you." Faith dashed down the stairs and out the door, continued to the avenue, and hailed a cab. She checked her watch: 9:20. No cab. She ran a few blocks, spotted a bagman asleep on the sidewalk, placed the breakfast near his head, ran to the avenue where there was a subway. Beads of sweat seeped into her eyes. Faith used her sleeve to dab the corners of her eyes, inhaled deeply, and trotted downstairs to the train station. She entered the platform. Five rows of straphangers. "Shit! Damn train." She immediately trotted to street level, ran for twenty blocks, stopped, reached in her bag for her pass, adjusted her sunglasses, and rushed to the elevator bank.

Faith's desk clock read 10:05 AM. She threw her bag under the desk, turned on her computer, and plopped into the chair. "Son of a bitch."

Joan smiled. Faith removed her jacket, tugged a Kleenex from her bag, and wiped sweat from her forehead. Joan whispered to Faith, "Had to run again, huh?"

Faith glared at Joan. "Yes, I did. You think I would lose a pound or two, but no."

Joan snickered.

Faith keyed in her name and password on her computer. She glanced at Joan. "Joan, what age was your son when he said his first words?"

"My son did not talk until he was five years old, and he has not stopped. Now, he's ten."

Guy pushed his cart into Faith's desk. "Hunter will be fine, he needs more time."

Faith plucked her hair brush out of her bag and bushed. Her hair stuck. "Shit." Faith untangled the brush from her hair and tossed it in the bag. "Well, I have an appointment with a therapist in one week. My kid's classification is autism, he's in therapy at two years old."

John's office door, opposite Faith's desk, opened. He stepped out and glanced up from his documents. Guy dropped the mail in the in-box. John leaned on Faith's shelf, read over a letter, made some edits, cleared his throat, and handed the document over to Faith. "Faith, make an appointment for yourself at the therapist while you are at it."

Faith snickered, "Sure."

John continued, "Please do these edits on the letter for me."

Faith reached for the document. "I'll do it right now."

John hesitated, leaned on her shelf, made more edits to another document. "Faith, could you also make these changes on this document, the letter takes priority, thank you." John returned to his office and shut the door.

Joan opened the newspaper. "Time to read the horoscopes, let's see, what's my day going to be like?"

Faith worked on the edits. "My day already sucks."

Joan kept on. "What's your sign again, Faith?"

Faith continued to edit. "Virgo. The best sign in the zodiac."

Joan repeated, "Virgo."

Guy rolled his cart near Faith's desk, placed a box on her shelf, and warned, "Better do that later, ladies. Mary is coming down the hall."

Faith quickly hid her food in the desk drawer and whispered, "Joan, what time did I come in this morning?"

Joan placed her paper under her desk. Guy rolled his cart out, past Mary. Joan whispered, "10:05, Faith."

Mary stood at attention. "Faith, may I see you in my office now please."

Faith faintly replied, "Okay."

Faith found it difficult to keep pace with Mary's angry walk. Mary held open her office door, Faith entered and took a seat in the guest chair. Mary continued, "Mr. Harold will be here momentarily."

Faith shivered at the iced words. "Mr. Harold?"

Mr. Harold entered and said, "Good morning, ladies."

Faith blinked back a few tears. "Good morning, Mr. Harold."

Mary rolled her chair into position behind her desk, glared sternly, shuffled contents of a file, and vehemently stated, "Faith, you have arrived late five times since our last meeting. I have also received several complaints from your attorneys regarding your work product."

Faith interrupted, "My work product? Who complained?"

Mr. Harold coughed and winked at Faith.

Mary interjected, "They all did."

Faith bowed her head for a moment, "Oh, so no one is happy." Mary said with a smile, "No, no one is happy."

Faith suggested, "Can I transfer to another department?"

Mary replied flatly, "No, we have no positions open at this time."

Mr. Harold held out a sealed envelope. "I have a check for you. This check includes all your time plus three weeks vacation."

Mary stood, reached across her desk, and seized the check.

Mr. Harold gave Mary a startled look. She spoke slowly, "Thank you Mr. Harold." Mary glared at Faith. "Faith, you have a bad attitude. Rules apply to you as well as others in this society—you're not above the law. Faith nodded in agreement and tried remove the envelope from Mary's grasp. Mary held tight and continued, "Rules are enforced to maintain uniformity, for everyone, Faith, not just a select few. Work should not be used to socialize. Remember this advice. Guy will escort you out."

Faith snatched the check as Mary reluctantly released her grip. Faith folded the envelope and slipped it in her bag. "Before you escort me out, I need a few things at my desk."

Mr. Harold responded, "We understand, Faith. This is procedure." Mr. Harold adjusted his tie while Mary viciously dialed Guy's extension.

"Guy, meet Faith at my office please."

Mr. Harold coughed. Mary intensely glared at Faith for several moments of uncomfortable silence. Then Faith spoke firmly, "Thanks. I'll be able to spend more time with my son. Thanks for this favor."

Mary's angry glare stabbed Faith between the eyes like a lightening bolt. Guy knocked at the door, and Mr. Harold smiled in relief. Faith left the office and shut the door. Faith walked with Guy down the hall and murmured with a smile, "She is such a bitch!"

Guy smiled, "Yep."

Faith threw shoes and pictures into a bankers box. Guy sadly commented, "Sorry, Faith."

Joan hugged her good-bye. "Keep in touch, Faith, if you ever need a roommate I know a good person you can trust to rent to."

Faith hugged Joan. "You can keep my snacks." Tissue in hand, Faith dabbed tears from her eyes.

Guy hoisted the box on his shoulder and said, "Faith, we better go."

Faith tapped the elevator button. Guy set the box down and hugged Faith. "Is this part of the procedure?"

Guy released the hug. "No." The elevator bonged, and the light flashed red. "Faith, there's the elevator to freedom."

Faith entered the elevator, pressed lobby, and waved good-bye to Guy.

Lobby security held open the door as Faith lugged the box out. She walked to the corner and dropped the box near the pay phone. She searched her bag for change, pushed the coins into the slot, and hit the digits on the dial pad. Balancing her bag on the phone rack, she lost her grip on the box, spilling its contents onto the sidewalk.

As Faith blinked back tears, a tissue appeared before her. "Thank you." Faith took the tissue from a woman who continued past. Faith spoke into the receiver, "Frank, please meet me outside my building. I got fired."

She hung up the phone, gathered the contents of the box, and dragged it over to the sidewalk bench. Pigeons edged close to the box. She kicked up her foot, and the pigeons fluttered down the block.

Frank arrived energetically. "Move over, bitch."

Faith pouted, "My life sucks. What am I going to do?"

Frank joined Faith on the bench and threw his arm around her. Faith leaned into his shoulder. "Take a vacation, Faith."

"Vacation? I just got fired, and I'm on a limited budget."

Frank inquired, "Faith, how much did you get?"

"Three weeks, my new personal best. I usually get banished after three months."

Frank smiled, "Not bad, three weeks. You were only there two months. You get three weeks, collect unemployment."

"Not enough hours in the unemployment kitty. I have a child to care for. I'd better get another job today."

Frank yanked his arm back, "It's hot enough today without you blowing more hot air. Go home and fire the sitter."

Faith placed her head in her hands and leaned over at the waist as if falling. "I just hired the sitter. Her husband works at the deli, he keeps a running tab for me. Now what? I'll fire his wife, I'll have to pay up."

Frank kissed Faith on the head and gave her a hug, "Call me, I've got to get back. Get up!" Frank hugged Faith. "You'll be okay."

"Sure, my kid has a disability, sure I'll be okay."

Frank shook Faith. "Stop it." Frank kissed her forehead and crossed the street.

Faith merged into the crowd. A stranger banged her shoulder, and the box dropped. Items bounced out and rolled along the sidewalk. People helped collect her things. "Thank God I left the gold pieces at home," she said, triggering snickers from the group.

Speech Therapy

THE BUZZ RELEASED THE locked door. Faith backed into the hallway, balancing the stroller in one arm, Hunter in the other. Hunter wriggled free and climbed into the bow window. A second buzzer opened the office. Faith jammed the stroller through the door, collected Hunter, and plopped him onto the couch in a waiting room that held an abundance of toys. He squirmed off the couch, landed in front of a dollhouse, and began to open and close the door. Faith zeroed in on an airplane and flew it over to Hunter. "Hunter, honey, look, the airplane has a door." No response from Hunter.

A young, casually dressed brunette entered the room with a welcoming smile. "Ms. Parker, I'm Carla. How are you?"

Faith smiled, "Hi, Carla, Faith Parker and this is Hunter."

Carla handed Faith some forms. "Please fill out these forms honestly. It will help in my evaluation."

"Sure, no problem. Hunter enjoys the 'shut the door' game."

Carla joined Hunter. "Please come into my office. I'll work with Hunter while you complete the forms."

Faith smiled. Carla took Hunter's hand. He peeked at Carla and pulled his hand away. Carla inched closer to the dollhouse and snatched it. Hunter followed Carla into her office. She pointed to her desk, and Faith made herself comfortable there. Carla led Hunter to a chair at the children's table.

Faith surveyed the room and commented, "Carla, this looks like my apartment."

Carla responded, "Lots of fun clutter, things we need." Carla placed the dollhouse on the table, tucked Hunter's chair tight against the table, and knelt beside him. Faith listened to Carla's narration of Hunter's actions, "Hunter open, Hunter close door, Hunter open door, Hunter close door." Hunter stimmed.

Faith handed the completed forms over to Carla, who skimmed through the papers. "I'll go over these tonight." She placed the forms on the corner of her desk. "Please, let's begin. We have to hold hands in a small circle."

Carla gently held Hunter's hand and sang, "Ring-around-the-rosy."

Hunter backed away from Carla, thrust himself at the door and hung on the doorknob. Faith slipped from behind the desk, "Hunter, that's a no. Come and sit."

Carla reached for Hunter's hands, lowered herself to his eye level, and sang, "Hunter, Hunter, away from the door, away from the door." Carla glanced at Faith. "Singing helps children like Hunter, you must sing slowly, very slowly, so that Hunter will understand the words."

Faith removed Hunter's hands from the doorknob and sat with him in the child-size chair. "I hope this doesn't break."

Carla smiled, "These chairs are very sturdy. Shall we try to sing ring-around-the-rosy?"

Faith cradled Hunter in her arms. "Sure."

Faith lowered Hunter to the floor. Carla held one of Hunter's hands and Faith held the other. They began to move in a circle. Faith sang out, "Hunter, h e r e w e g o r o u n d t h e m u l b e r r y b u s h, t h e m u l b e r r y b u s h."

Carla looked at Faith questioningly. "We are singing r i n g-a r o u n d-t h e-r o s y."

"Oh, sorry."

Hunter yanked his hands free and hung on the doorknob. Faith wrapped her arms around Hunter and tugged him into her lap. She sang, "Hunter, f i r s t t h e s o n g, t h e n g o." Hunter placed his hand over Faith's mouth.

Carla unhooked the closet door and opened it to reveal a throng of toys. She selected a giant bubble blower. Blown bubbles caught Hunter's attention, he stimmed. A bubble floated in front of Faith, she reached out, it popped. Carla and Hunter felt the moist spray, "Sorry, guys."

Hunter body slammed Faith. "Oh my, Hunter, take it easy!"

Carla reached for the ball under the desk and said to Faith, "You must do a lot of floor time." Carla rolled the ball to Hunter, who was secured in Faith's lap. She said, "Please, Mom, place Hunter's hand on the ball, roll the ball back to me."

Faith placed her hand over Hunter's hand on the ball and rolled the ball to Carla. Hunter stimmed.

Faith instructed, "Hunter, roll ball."

Carla slid over, placed Hunter's hands on the ball, and, together they pushed it to Faith. Faith pushed the ball back. It stopped beside Hunter. He stared at the ball,

Carla coached Faith, "Speak in one or two word phrases."

Faith reached for the ball, "B a l l, mi n e."

Carla commented, "That's great."

Hunter leaped high and beelined for the computer on Carla's desk. He slammed his little fist on the keyboard.

"N o, H u n t e r, n o. " Carla intercepted Hunter's hand to prevent the next fist slam on the keyboard, and she guided him away from the computer. "No, Hunter. Hunter has had enough for today, Mom."

Faith bear hugged Hunter, and, enclosing him in her arms, asked, "Carla, specifically, what should I work on with him?"

Carla placed a cover over her computer. "Floor time is very important, a lot of interaction, work with Hunter so he will understand response, do exactly the exercises we were doing today. Another helpful task is to take pictures or cut out pictures of his favorite foods and paste them on paper. Keep the cut-outs in a loose–leaf binder. Hunter must show you the picture first before he gets, say, popcorn or pizza. This develops association."

"Okay, thanks, Carla."

Carla added, "Hunter needs organization to help him visually, to see that everything has a place."

Faith kissed Hunter's cheek. "No problem, thank you." Faith opened the door. Hunter ran down the hall. Faith opened the second door, and Hunter rushed to lie in the bow window. He covered his eyes from the sun's glare.

Park Battles

FAITH CHASED HUNTER THROUGH the park. "How about the swing? Hunter, S w i n g!!"

A toddler girl holding Elmo in her lap rolled by. Hunter seized Elmo and ran. The child's mother hollered, "Excuse me, that's my daughter's."

Faith blocked Hunter, excused his actions, "Sorry, sorry, Hunter, give back."

The mother snapped, "Manners are important to teach a child."

"I agree."

The woman grabbed Elmo from Hunter's hands and retreated to the opposite end of the park. Hunter dropped to the ground and yelped. Adults in the area observed suspiciously. Faith spoke into the air, "He's my little crowd pleaser." She knelt beside Hunter. "Hunter, we have other things to play with in the park."

Faith gathered Hunter into her arms, rushed over to the sandbox, settled Hunter in the middle, scooped a handful of sand, and sifted the sand through her fingers. "Look, Hunter, s a n d."

Hunter stimmed, focused on the falling sand for a few moments, then spotted a silver car, abandoned, buried under dirt. He reached for the silver car, flipped it over, and spun the wheels. He marched around the box with Faith's help, collecting the abandoned cars and trucks. Then, he lined them up in a row and stimmed.

From the park benches, an audience of elders pointed at Hunter. Faith directed her comment toward them, "He was a car salesman in his previous life." Some giggled, others turned away.

Hunter stimmed, Faith gave him a big kiss and hug. "Mommy loves her little caveman."

Faith held Hunter directly in front of her eyes, forcing eye contact. Hunter turned away with closed eyes. "Little man, we'll have to work on your eye contact. Hey, caveman, get in the stroller." Hunter climbed in and held his hand out. Faith kissed his hand.

"Say the word j u i c e!" Hunter grabbed the bottle and gulped. Faith rolled the stroller out of the park.

Happenstance

FAITH RELEASED HUNTER'S STROLLER seat belt before they got to hardware store. A tall, dark haired, tightly toned man held the door open. Faith smiled, "Thanks!"

He responded, "You're welcome."

The manager switched the radio station from the news to oldies music, leaned on his cash register, and watched his customers mill about the store.

Faith asked, "Excuse me, where can I find shelves?"

"Aisle three."

The same man who had held the door open greeted Faith in aisle three with a smile. She returned the smile and checked on Hunter. He had converged on the plugs, stripped them from the shelf, and placed them in a straight line middle of the aisle.

Casually, she inched closer to the man. "Excuse me, do you think this is more practical than this fixture?"

He smiled, "What will the shelf be supporting?"

Faith laughed, "Toys mostly, some children's books." Faith checked on Hunter again. He had discovered the sponges, removed them from the shelf, placed them middle of the aisle.

The man questioned, "You are doing this yourself?"

Faith did not make eye contact. "Yes. I have all the tools, the molly fasteners," she said, displaying the contents of her basket.

The man shifted his weight from one leg to another. "I recognize you from the deli. You're Faith, right?"

"Yeah that's me. The deli, which deli?"

"Across the street. Your son blocked doorway—no one could get in or out. He seemed to be hypnotized by the blinking lights on the deli sign."

Smiles were traded.

Faith responded, "Sorry, were you in a rush?"

Nervously, he twirled his keys around in his hand. "No, no not at all, just heard your name, remembered it."

Faith smiled, "Your name is?"

"Dave, my name is Dave," he glanced up at the ceiling, looked directly into Faith's eyes.

Faith swooped Hunter up in one arm and picked up the supplies in the other. "Well, thanks for your help." They again traded smiles. She headed for the checkout. Hunter squirmed out of Faith's grasp at the register and dashed back to the sponge aisle. Faith dropped the money on the counter and quickly retrieved Hunter. Dave arrived behind Faith in the checkout line. They again traded smiles. Dave took the shelves from Faith and helped carry them outside. Hunter screamed during the exit, and, outside, the bright sunshine forced him to cover his eyes with his hands.

Faith said, "Thanks. I'll take the shelves." She adjusted her supplies. Dave put on his sunglasses. "He certainly is not shy about screaming."

Faith placed Hunter in the stroller, but Hunter climbed back out.

"Faith, would you be interested in a job?"

She balanced the shelves on the stroller, thought for a moment. "A job? You can tell I'm unemployed?" Faith placed the shelves on the sidewalk, Hunter climbed in the stroller, and Faith fastened the seat belt.

Dave scribbled down information on a piece of torn bag. "I'm always impressed with a woman who can handle tools." Dave pointed to a building, "That building across the street—you get a hundred dollars, off the books."

Faith smirked, accepted the offer, and placed the piece of paper in the hardware bag. Hunter pointed toward the deli. Faith laughed, "We have to go, Dave. What time do I start?"

Dave anxiously fired back, "Nine o'clock. Apartment three-J."

Faith balanced the shelves on the stroller, rolled across the street, and shouted, "I'll be there. Thanks."

Dave waved and smiled. Faith readjusted her supplies and headed for the deli.

She parked the stroller outside the deli. Sam came out the door, "How's my wife working out?"

Faith unhooked Hunter's seat belt. "She's wonderful, Sam."

Sam gently tapped Hunter's head. Hunter pushed his hand away. "You don't need her today?"

Faith smiled, "No. We had an appointment. Sam, you know a guy Dave, a carpenter Dave?"

Sam scratched his stomach, untied his apron, "Dave, Dave, oh yeah, he hires girls to help him out."

Hunter scooted into the deli. "Does he pay?" Faith followed Hunter.

Sam followed Faith. "Oh yeah, he pays." Sam smiled. "He asked you to work?"

Faith threw some chips on the counter. Hunter stimmed at the spinning advertisement in the window. "He did. Should I do it?"

Sam rang up the items. "Of course. I'll tell Lila to be there early, eight thirty in the morning. Three-fifty please."

Hunter flew out the door and hopped into his stroller. On the way out, Faith said, "Sam, please put that on my tab."

Organization

HUNTER REWOUND AND REPLAYED his favorite scene. Frank looked over his shoulder. "Jeez. Is that all he does all day?"

Faith pulled the pencil from her ear. "Yep."

Hunter rewound the scene, played the scene, rewound, played.

Frank held the shelf brace, and Faith marked the place with pencil. Frank drilled the screw into the wall and gently let go of the brace, and they both took a step back to observe.

"Well, is it straight?"

"It looks straight to me, Frank."

Hunter stationed himself in front of the television, his feet covered in Kleenex. Frank clicked off the television and said, "Enough of that!"

Hunter rebelled and clicked the television back on. Frank pulled out a tissue from the Kleenex box and dropped it over Hunter's head. Hunter grabbed the Kleenex, tossed it higher above his head, and watched the tissue float through the air.

"See, Faith, he likes to watch the Kleenex fall."

Faith spoke slowly, "K L E E N E X, Hunter, K L E E N E X." The tissue swirled slowly to the floor as Hunter replayed his specific scene. He paused, took a tissue from the Kleenex box, stood on the futon, dropped the tissue, and watched it float to the floor. Faith commented, "Great.

Look at what you are teaching him to do." She pointed to the unfinished shelf.

"Oh, is that my cue?"

"Yes it is."

Frank slammed the hammer on his thumb. "Bitch, hold him steady." He dropped the hammer to the floor and shook his hand. "***Ouch!*** This work is too macho for me." Frank flopped on the futon. "Jeez, it's hot in here!"

Faith laughed. "Work will make you sweat."

Frank frowned, "It's summer, turn up the air!"

Faith said encouragingly, "You're doing a great job." Hunter leaped from the futon into Faith's arms. "Ouch!!" she exclaimed. Faith carried Hunter over to Frank and told him, "Hunter, kiss his thumb, make it better."

As Hunter jumped onto the futon, his leg hit Frank's leg hard. Frank rolled off the futon. "Brat!" He grabbed a tennis ball from the floor, limped to place it on the shelf. It rolled down the shelf and bounced on the floor. Frank shook his head at Faith.

There was a bang, then a buzz of the door bell. Frank shrugged. "Who's at your door?" he asked.

Faith replied, "It's the neighbor."

Frank added sarcastically, "What!"

Faith pointed to the ball. "Too much noise." She continued, "My neighbor's a complainer."

Frank stood with his hands on his hips. "What!"

Faith hurried through the kitchen and opened the door with a cheerful, "Hi."

The neighbor was wrapped tightly in a green robe, her hair a messy mop, wearing her faded pink slippers. She cleared her throat. "I hear a buzzing and a ball bouncing. I am trying to rest."

"We'll keep it down." Faith closed the door with, "Have a good day."

Faith laughed at Frank's distressed glare. "Did you get rid of her?"

Faith laughed, "Of course. She's such a nuisance."

Frank again rolled the ball down the shelf. "Did you measure?"

Faith plopped on the futon. "Well I measured, but, you know."

Frank said, "The shelf's secure. Too late to change it now. Some assistant you'll make. You took the clutter from the floor to the shelf. What is all this shit?"

Faith laughed, "This is part of his therapy. Hunter has to have organization."

Frank shrugged. "I know what a shelf does. What's that?" Frank pointed to a book on the floor with taped pictures of food.

Faith explained, "Hunter must point to the picture of what he wants, we say the word together, then he is rewarded. Hunter, are you hungry?"

Hunter stimmed and rocked, focused on the animation. Faith leaned over and showed Hunter the food pictures. Frank snatched the book and flipped through the pages. "Do you have all this in your refrigerator?" he asked.

Faith stole back the book back. "No. I'm waiting until he wants something, then I'll buy it."

Frank fired back, "Give me the number three to go."

Hunter grabbed the book and tossed it out into the kitchen. Frank observed, "That's what he thinks of your book."

Hunter rewound the scene, tapped play, and stimmed. Faith was annoyed. "Can we finish with the shelf?"

Frank pointed to the drill. "Hand over the drill. You sure this guy Dave doesn't just want to drill you?"

Faith smiled, "He's very cute."

Frank picked up the drill. "Be sure to call me with the details at lunch tomorrow. Ask for the money up front in case you measure improperly."

Faith said, "I'm testing out a new career, see if I like carpentry."

Frank drilled a hole in the wall, and the bit jammed. "This is not a good sign." He squeezed the trigger. No energy. "Time to recharge," he said.

Faith opened the drill case. "Where's the charger?"

Frank laughed, "You'll meet the charger tomorrow."

Faith searched for the charger under the bed. "You are a pig. There it is by the television!"

Faith yanked the drill from the wall, attached it to the charger, and plugged it into the socket. Frank swooped up Hunter, held him high, then swung him down to the bed. He sat with Hunter on the futon.

Faith squeezed between them and asked, "What are you watching?"

Frank turned off the TV. "Nothing!" Hunter stomped over clicked on the TV.

Carpenter's Assistant

FAITH WIGGLED HER NOSE and stared into the light to prevent a sneeze she felt erupting. Dave drilled the sheet rock to the wall. "Steady," he said. Dave swung the drill and pointed to a wide board on the opposite side of the room.

Faith snickered, "You could communicate with my son."

Dave walked toward the plank and asked, "What are you talking about?"

Faith wiped the sweat from her forehead with the back of her hand. She replied, "You point like my son does, not much verbalization."

Dave lifted one side. "Faith, help me bring this upstairs."

"Sure." Faith took her place on the opposite side.

"On three, we'll lift and carry this across the room."

Faith squatted and lifted her side of the board. Dave hauled his side and passed a thunderous fart. Overcome with laughter, Faith dropped her side of the board. Dave dropped his side. "What are you laughing at?"

Faith asked between laughs, "Did you hear that?"

Dave leaned on the wall. "No, I heard nothing."

Faith couldn't control herself. She inhaled. "Really, are you sure? Do you smell that?"

Dave backed away from Faith, irritated. "No I don't. Faith, let's get back to work, lift the board, please, we have to get this done."

Faith regained her composure, lifted her end, and walked backwards upstairs. They placed the board on the floor. Faith spoke up, "It was you."

Dave's mood lightened. "No, no I thought it was you!"

Faith retorted, "I only fart internally."

Dave laughed heartily, "I've never heard of internal farts!" Dave bowed his head toward the wall. "Go, Faith, go. You are stronger after the fart."

Faith squatted and elevated her side while Dave boosted his side. Faith's hand slipped, and the board slammed into her fingers against the floor. She cried out, "Help, the board in on my hand."

Dave yanked the board off of Faith's scraped her fingers and said, "Shit."

Faith wrapped her fingers in a small crumpled Kleenex that she had in her pocket. She cried out, "Pain, pain." She stripped off her white shirt and wrapped it around her bleeding hand.

Dave insisted, "Go to the bathroom." They rushed to the bathroom, where Dave helped wash off her hand and administered first aid.

Faith cried, "***Stop! Ooooh.***"

A door slammed open. A blonde, petite, pregnant woman entered, bristling with defiance. "You son of a bitch. Who's this whore?"

Faith, startled by her presence, spoke up. "I cut my hand." She held up her finger.

Dave babbled, "Angel, her hand is cut."

Tears rolled down Angel's face, "You bastard."

Angel thrust past and regurgitated into the toilet.

Faith exited with her hand wrapped in a towel. Dave followed. Faith spoke quietly, "When my son gets very upset he throws up."

Dave quipped, "She's pregnant, Faith."

Faith picked up her bag and said, "You are in big trouble. Time for me to go."

Dave dug in his pocket. "Please, take this." He handed Faith a hundred dollars.

"Thank you." Faith turned back. "Hey, Dave, can I use you as a reference?"

"Any time." Dave returned to the bathroom.

Faith held her injured hand and trotted down the stairs, heading to the park.

Dodging mammoth squirt guns, swift scooters, and strollers at the park's entrance, Faith searched for her caveman. Hunter stood alone under the sprinkler, stimming. Lila waited just beyond the water's spray with an open towel. Faith waved to Lila. Lila called to her, "Faith, he does not want to leave."

Faith ran through the sprinkler, swung Hunter into her arms, and wrapped him in the towel. "The water's freezing, Lila." Hunter wrestled free, returned to the sprinkler, stimmed.

Lila commented, "When Hunter's cold, he runs to the sandbox and rolls in the hot sand, then returns the to water. What happened to your hand?"

Faith showed her the wound, "I cut it on the job. My carpenter career is over."

Lila took Faith's hand gently. "Let me see that. It's gross." Lila examined it. She asked, "Does it need a stitch?"

Faith took her hand back, "Oh, it's okay. Thanks, Lila." She shouted, "Hunter, Hunter! Hello!"

Lila interrupted, "Faith, I have to return to my home for a while, my father is sick."

Faith replied sorrowfully, "I'm sorry to hear that."

Lila continued, "I will be gone for a month, perhaps more."

Faith gave Lila a hug. "I am sorry your Dad is not well." Hunter bolted to the other side of the park. Faith called "Hunter! Lila, like he listens, where's he going?"

Lila laughed, "He likes to watch the people get on and off the bus." Faith caught up to Hunter at the bench, which had a great view of the bus stop. He was stimming. Lila followed with the stroller. Hunter climbed into his stroller seat. Lila threw the towel over him. Faith strolled beside as Lila pushed the carriage. Hunter tossed the towel off his lap. Faith laughed and swooped the towel off the ground.

Love Dogs

HUNTER CLIMBED THE TREE that bordered the edge of the sidewalk and yanked down a skinny branch. Faith hugged his waist and tugged him away from the branch. "Let go of the tree, Hunter. I have a cookie for you."

Hunter released the branch. It swished, and he stimmed. Faith unwrapped an Oreo cookie pack from her bag. She placed an Oreo cookie on her head. "Hunter, look at Mommy." Hunter focused on the Oreo. Faith demanded, "Look into Mommy's eyes."

Hunter briefly held eye contact and grabbed the cookie. "One at a time, Hunter." He twisted the Oreo cookie top until it separated from the cream. He licked the cream off and tossed the chocolate top to the ground. Faith sipped her juice as she observed his technique. Hunter rocked, chewed, stimmed. A group of dogs approached. Hunter greeted them with a tug on the ear. Faith smiled at the dog walker and checked out his broad shoulders, strong arms, and thick brown hair. She watched him yank a piece of paper out of his pants pocket. The dogs were silent as he reviewed his list.

The largest dog leaned over, stretched out his tongue, and licked Hunter from his chin to his forehead with a slurp. Hunter squealed with delight. "Bear, stop that and sit," barked the walker. The dogs barked. "Everybody, quiet." They obeyed; he rattled his circular key ring and made a selection. He smiled at Hunter, "Do you have a dog, young fella?"

Faith answered for Hunter, gazing into the man's deep blue eyes, "No, not yet, but he loves dogs." Faith smiled and offered the walker a cookie.

He shook his head no, and responded, "No dogs." He took his card from his back pocket and handed it to Faith, "Here's my card. If you should get a dog, I'll walk him. Reasonable rates."

Faith reviewed and commented, "Well, Mr. North Smyth, do you do the hiring? I'm interested in a part-time job."

Mr. Smyth squatted beside Faith on the stoop as he delivered his response with a grand smile, "What hours are you available?" He winked.

Hunter positioned himself in the midst of the dogs. One nudged Hunter's hair with his nose. Faith returned the wink. "From about 9:00 AM until 4:00 PM." She caught sight of his muscular thighs as she read the card and commented, "Tight Leash, a great name."

North nodded his head in agreement. "How much do you want an hour?"

Faith blurted out "Twenty dollars per hour." Hunter screamed, and a few dogs retreated. North flexed his strong tanned arms and picked up Hunter. He passed him over to Faith, asking, "You're not afraid of big aggressive dogs?"

Faith held Hunter in her lap. "I love big aggressive dogs."

North laughed out loud, "When can you start?"

Faith kissed Hunter, he wriggled out of her lap. "How about next week?"

North responded, "Monday, great. Your name is?"

Faith stood and shook hands with North. "Faith Parker."

North spoke authoritatively, "Faith Parker, I'll meet you here Monday morning at 10:00 AM."

"Great." They froze, smiling, hands still clasped.

North broke the hold, "Excuse me, I have to run inside to pick up my client."

North entered the lobby. Faith checked out his butt, exhaled, "Wow!" She slipped North's card into her pocket and commanded, "Hunter, stop! Do not lick the big dog's face. Time to go inside."

Faith gently tapped all the hounds' heads and got a lick, a nudge of their noses on her hand. She bear hugged Hunter, and he laughed. They entered the lobby, and she waved to North down the hall, "See you tomorrow." Faith carried Hunter up the stairs.

Room For Rent

FAITH'S ARMS WERE FULL of clothes from her closet. She crossed over to the opposite bedroom and tossed her bundle on the bed. Frank rolled the ball to Hunter in the kitchen. Hunter stimmed, and the ball rolled past him. Frank reached for the ball with his foot and rolled it toward Hunter. It rolled into Faith's feet, tripping her. She slammed into the wall, dropping her second load of clothes and hangers on the floor, and tumbled onto the pile, shouting, "Hey, watch it."

Frank leaped to the rescue. "Sorry. I have a bad feeling. A roommate is not the best idea. What if you get some psycho in here?" Frank helped Faith off the floor.

Faith responded, "A co-worker recommended her friend; it's not a stranger."

Frank backed away from Faith, held Hunter by his waist, and swung him high over his head. As he lowered him to the floor quickly, he said, "Hunter, weeee, do you know your mom has a screw loose? Dog walking, ewww, those beasts shit and piss all over the street."

Faith lifted the pile from the floor and plopped the clothing on the bed. "Frank, I've been on the job for a month. Walking dogs is a lot of work but I bring Hunter with me. Don't you have any faith in me?"

Frank held Hunter over his head, and Hunter squealed with delight.

Frank lowered him to the floor, answering, "I know you too well. Track down Hunter's father. Money would help your situation."

Faith shook her head and rolled her eyes. "I told him I was pregnant with a girl, and I never heard from him again. Obviously he isn't curious."

"Obviously, the truth may be in order here." Frank rolled the ball to Hunter. Hunter stimmed as the ball passed his feet. Frank picked up a few hangers handed them to Faith.

She said, "Oh yeah, that."

Frank pulled the ball back with his foot. "Don't be a bitch."

Faith slapped her wardrobe hangers onto the rack. "Stone told me it wouldn't matter what the sex was."

Frank kicked the ball "Stone is a liar."

Faith eyed Frank. "If this plan proves to be a failure, I'll try to contact him, how is that?"

The ball ricocheted off the wall and bounced off of Faith's head. Faith glared at Frank; Hunter clicked on the television. Frank grabbed the ball and said, "Plans, plans, Hunter, oh, Hunter, plan on meeting your father very soon."

The door bell buzzed. Both Faith and Frank jumped. Faith blurted, "My first landlord–tenant meeting. Are you ready?"

Frank took Hunter onto his lap on the kitchen chair. "Bring him in." Faith opened the door and waited in the hall. Frank whispered to Faith, "He'll say, 'isn't this cozy?'"

Faith fired Frank a shut-up look. She greeted the visitor, "Hi, how are you? I'm Faith. Joan told me your name but I've forgotten, sorry." Faith shook his hand.

"My name is Jack Heart."

Faith stepped back into the apartment and invited, "Please come in, Jack. Nice to meet you."

Jack stood at the threshold and nodded hello to Frank. "Joan said you had worked together in the past." Jack smiled at Hunter.

"Yes we did. Joan is a good person." Faith stood next to Frank. "Jack, I just want to warn you, the place is small, and the tub is in the kitchen. You'd have a separate bedroom with a door to close for privacy, your own telephone, TV with cable, and a view of the street."

Jack smiled, "Sounds good. You're in a great location."

Frank squeezed Hunter to keep him controlled, and he observed Jack from behind. Jack was a tall man of six feet with broad shoulders; a slim waist; and long, thick hair. His smiled widened. Faith winked and gave the 'hot' sign. Frank's eyes locked on Jack.

Faith paused, coughed, and nudged Frank. "You remember Joan from my office?" she asked. "This is her friend."

Frank balanced Hunter on his left hip and extended his hand for a welcome handshake. "Very nice to meet you. This young man's Hunter. Watch out—he's a thief."

Faith interrupted, "Frank, he's not a thief!"

Jack touched Hunter's head gently and said, "Very nice to meet you. I have something for you, Hunter." Jack handed Hunter a shiny keychain with a small ball attached.

Faith said excitedly, "Isn't that nice! Thanks! Please check out the room." Faith opened the bedroom door. "Come in please."

Faith ogled Jack as he leaned over the futon and pushed down on the mattress. "Will this hold up?"

Faith laughed, "Up to three hundred pounds. If you don't like the white spread, let me know."

Jack opened the closet and touched the bar. It rolled to the back of the closet. "Can I build shelves?" he asked.

Faith smiled, "Sure."

Jack slid over to the window, pulled the curtain back, and smiled. "Just so you know, I'm not a nine-to-five person. I sleep a little later in the morning and come in late at night. Is that a problem with the baby?"

Faith used the remote to click on the television. "No, no problem," she replied. "The main rule is, please just yourself—no guests, no one-night stands."

Jack winked. "Just me. I understand." Faith felt her temperature rise and hoped her face wasn't red.

Frank grumbled from the kitchen, "The rent is two hundred dollars per week."

Faith silently mouthed "Quiet" to Frank, then said, "Jack, I'll leave you to think, I'll just close the door for privacy." Faith paused for another gander at Jack. He checked his cell phone, used the remote to flip channels, opened the gate, stepped out on the fire escape, and spoke on his cell.

Faith closed the door and twirled into the kitchen. Hunter sat on top of the table, crunching a muffin with his hands.

Frank gripped Faith's arm. "Where's the new tenant?"

Faith smiled, "Jack, the hottie, is on the fire escape making a call."

Frank said authoritatively, "Be careful, Faith. Why would a hot number like that need a room?"

Faith laughed, "Wow, Joan never mentioned how handsome. Plus, he got a trinket for Hunter."

Frank grabbed the keychain. "He gave him something he could choke on."

The creak of the floor alerted them of Jack's approach. "Here he comes. Will you please relax? It's just temporary, Frank."

Frank advised, "Ask for a month up front."

The door opened, and they both smiled to welcome Jack into the kitchen.

Jack stood with money in hand. "Faith, I have four hundred dollars for the remainder of the month. If it's all right, I'd like to move in tomorrow." Jack placed four one-hundred dollar bills on the table.

Frank's and Faith's eyes widened at the new hundred-dollar bills. Hunter threw his arms over his head, standing in front of Jack. Jack raised Hunter to his shoulders. Frank held Hunter's hand and seductively inched closer to Jack. He said flirtatiously, "Hunter likes you, Jack."

Jack leaned away from Frank and commented, "Kids and dogs love me."

Faith counted the money as Frank inspected Jack. Faith spoke up. "Jack, I do love money but I'd prefer the rent weekly, just in case things do not work out. If we find it works we can renegotiate, okay?" Faith handed two hundred dollars back.

Jack took the money. "No problem." He passed Hunter back to Frank.

Frank focused on Jack's front pants area watching as Jack slipped the returned bills into his front pants pocket. Frank licked his lips. Jack moved near the door, away from Frank, Faith searched drawers. She slammed the top drawer shut, opened the middle drawer, searched, slammed the drawer shut, opened the third drawer, and found what she was looking for. She held up the keys, and Jack reached for them.

Frank asked with a wide grin, "How do you know Joan?"

Jack responded, "Joan's my cousin."

Faith hesitantly smiled, "Joan never mentioned that." Hunter wiggled out of Frank's arms. Faith continued, "Okay, so tomorrow you move in, you have the keys."

Jack held the keys up. "Thanks."

Frank slipped behind Jack, licked his lips, and watched Jack slide the keys into his back pocket. Frank smiled radiantly, examining Jack's perfect butt.

Jack flinched uncomfortably and checked his watch. "Faith, does it matter what time?"

Faith smiled, "Anytime during the daylight hours is fine." Faith opened the door to the hallway. Frank fake-pinched Jack's butt, and Faith rolled her eyes at Frank, but Jack missed all insinuation. Faith blocked Hunter's exit into the hall, holding him tightly in her arms.

Jack offered, "Faith I'll call you before I move."

Faith smiled, "Wonderful."

Jack trotted sideways down the stairs. Faith, Hunter, and Frank stood in the hall, listening as the footsteps faded. Faith closed the door, "Frank, I can't believe you."

Frank sat on the kitchen chair and fanned himself with his hand.

Faith sat opposite him and said, "He is fine soon to be mine."

"Now, wait a minute missy."

Hunter clicked on the power for the television. When Frank turned up the volume, Hunter pushed Frank away from the television with a scream. Frank covered his ears, and Faith laughed.

Dog Park Afternoon

PAWS CLICKED ON THE pavement; grunts, growls, and playful barks filled the dog run.

Faith relaxed with Hunter on a bench as North kept the ball rolling for his clients. "Faith, do you think you could board a couple of dogs this weekend?"

Faith helped Hunter throw a tennis ball. "Board a couple of dogs? Are you serious?"

The ball hit North on his back. "Ow! They're small dogs."

Faith responded, "It's a holiday, and I have a tenant."

North stopped mid-throw. "What?"

Faith threw a ball and replied, "A roommate."

Bothered, North continued, "A roommate? You got a roommate?" North handed off the ball to Hunter saying, "Throw the ball."

Hunter placed it on the ground. Dogs panted with their tongues out, waiting for someone to throw the ball. Faith picked up the ball and said, "Yes."

North anxiously took the ball from Faith and picked up a leash. "Man or woman?"

Faith rolled her eyes, "What does it matter to you?"

North chucked the ball. "I just asked! Don't get all bent out of shape.

Did you check out his references? You don't want a serial killer in the house."

Faith showed Hunter how to roll the ball, "He was referred by a friend I used to work with. He has been my roommate for three weeks already. We're going week-to-week in case it doesn't work out."

North kicked the ball to the opposite corner and hooked the dog leash to the fence. "Your roommate will probably be away. What kind of work does this guy do?"

Faith leashed dogs and tied them to the fence. "He pays the rent."

North herded more dogs together and tied the leashed dogs to the fence. "Let me know if he gives you trouble, I'll beat him up for you."

Faith laughed, "If he doesn't pay the rent, we'll sic the dogs on him."

North continued persuasively, "Faith, please, I've already confirmed with the owners that I would take the dogs on the fourth. There will be trouble for me unless you take Sleepy and Face this weekend. I'll give you fifty bucks extra. What do you say?"

Faith held Hunter's hand as she gathered the last two dogs. "Sleepy and Face, do they get along?" A small poodle sat near Hunter. He kissed the dog and laughed.

North opened the gate and exited, answering vaguely, "Of course."

Faith pushed the poodle away from Hunter and guided her leashed dogs out. "Are you going to the fireworks on the Fourth of July?"

North yelled over his shoulder tersely, "None of your business."

Faith stared at the back of North's head, "Why can't you share where you are going?"

North turned his group around to face Faith. "I've got something personal to do. Will you take the dogs?"

Faith insisted, "Tell me. What personal business you have?"

North exhaled. "I'm going to visit my mother."

Faith was jerked forward by the dogs, and she tripped over a leash, wobbled, fought to regain her balance with several giant steps, and caught herself. "Oh, you have a mother. You never mentioned her."

Hunter stomped on Tenant's paw; the dog yelped and ran, with Hunter in hot pursuit. North leashed his canines to a bench and assisted Faith in retrieving Hunter. He teased, "Everybody has a mother. Or a Mother."

North picked up Hunter and placed him near Faith. She said, "Don't swear in front of Hunter. I'll do it for seventy dollars."

North returned to his dogs and petted them. "That's a bit steep, How about sixty?"

"Deal."

North headed to the street. "Great, I'll have their owners drop them at your place at about seven."

Faith confirmed, "Seven PM. Great, the roommate will not be home." Hunter hopped into the moving stroller. Faith paused and handed Hunter his bottle.

North demanded, "Did you sign up with Social Security? You may not need a roommate. They will help you financially with Hunter."

Faith wound the leashes around her wrist. "Monday, in two weeks, I need the day off."

North smiled, "So you do listen. For that, yes."

Together, North and Faith herded their beasts across the street, then split up on the other side.

Jack at Home

JACK, SURROUNDED BY DOGS, admired his handy work as he reached for the drill to secure some bolts. He gently nudged the dogs away, and they obliged, their tails wagging. "Good dogs. Sit, good boys, sit. Don't put your nose in there."

Hearing an obnoxious bang at the door, Jack silenced the barks with dog treats, gave Hunter a love tap in the tub, and opened the front door.

Wrapped in her green robe, wearing black slippers, and holding a cell phone, the neighbor blurted her complaint, "I'm trying to rest, and all I hear are dogs barking and a hum. Please stop the noise." Jack flashed his sexy smile. She ignored the smile, gave him the once over, and demanded, "Quiet, please," then swung around to her apartment and slammed the door.

Jack gently guided the hounds away from the door, filled a cup with water and poured the cup over Hunter's head as he stimmed. The door buzzer screeched. Jack pushed the door button, and Faith barreled in with Bear, Curly, Tenant, and Sam.

She leaned over to give Hunter a kiss. "How's my little man? Hunter likes his bath!" Hunter laughed at the word "bath."

Faith used a towel to wipe the sweat off her arms. "It's so hot out today." She touched Jack's arm, adding, "This is a big help to me, Jack, thank you."

Jack scooped a small rubber duck from the table, tossed it toward the tub. The duck was intercepted by Curly, who ran into Jack's room.

Silver-boy, another of the dogs, leaped at Hunter. Hunter grabbed Silver-boy's snout and laughed when the dog sneezed.

Jack replied sincerely, "No problem, love to help. Chicken nuggets are the special for this evening, would you like one?" Jack placed nuggets on a plate and hit the microwave timer for three minutes.

Silver-boy jumped beside the tub again, and again, Hunter grabbed his snout and laughed when the dog sneezed.

Faith pushed Silver-boy away. "Hunter you must stop that, don't hurt Silver-boy. We have to return him in one piece."

Curly returned to the kitchen and posed with duck still in his mouth. Faith snatched it and dropped the duck in the tub. She asked, "Who wants music? Hunter, dogs, here we go." Faith turned on the CD player and selected screen visuals to accompany the music—flashes of a variety of shapes and colors bounced to the beat, Hunter stimmed. Bear rose on his hind legs, placed his paws on Faith's back and knocked her into Jack's arms. Bear wagged his tail and barked. Faith lingered in Jack's strong arms for a moment as he help her stand, "Thanks, Jack, you're so strong to be able to hold me up."

"Subtract that from the rent."

Faith murmured, "That save was worth ten dollars." She hugged Bear, and he howled in time with the music.

Jack took a plate from the dish drainer, opened the microwave, and put the chicken nuggets on the plate. Bear nudged Jack's arm, then licked up fallen nuggets.

Faith laughed, "Down, Bear, that was dinner!" They opened the refrigerator and grabbed more nuggets.

Interrupted

Dogs huddled close together on a mattress in the center of the kitchen floor. They guarded Hunter; he controlled the television. Keys clicked, and Bear let out a low growl and nosed the door, assisted by Silver-boy, Curly, and Stanley. Noses at the door, their tails wagged. Hunter stimmed and rocked close to the television. Jack quietly opened the door and tossed in dog treats. Hunter slurped a treat in his mouth. "That's not for you, little buddy, give it back!" Jack called to Hunter and retrieved the biscuit from Hunter's mouth, then passed the biscuit to Stanley.

Canines scattered across the kitchen to eat their biscuits. Hunter raised his arms over his head, and Jack placed him on his shoulders, saying, "Caveman, what are you doing up? Back to bed you go." Jack carried Hunter to Faith's room. "Shh! we have to whisper! Your Mom's asleep. We'll slip you into bed, be very quiet." Jack peeked in at Faith, who was asleep. He entered, carefully placed Hunter beside her, covered Hunter, and kissed his forehead. Startled by the brightness of the computer's screen, Jack read, "Autism: The Signs; Mercury and Autism."

Jack glanced at Faith, asleep. He reviewed the screen, read what percentage of mercury stored in the body can cause damage. "Not good," he muttered. He checked out the multiplication figures on the notepad—

tuna, once per day, times three hundred and sixty-five days, times seven years, Jack shook his head, clicked the computer off, and slipped out. The door clicked closed.

Faith opened her eyes, hugged Hunter, and kissed him. "Mommy loves Hunter." Faith drew Hunter tightly to herself and let her tears fall onto Hunter's hair. Hunter touched Faith's cheek with his little hand. Faith kissed all his small fingers and waited. His breathing became heavy. She reached for the tissues by the bed and dried her eyes. Faith swung out of bed, tiptoed close to the door, and listened. Paws tapped on the kitchen floor, and a door squeaked, "Yeah! Jack took the dogs out." Faith lay still beside her son and whispered, "Baby, I'm sorry I ate so much fish, I loved fish, I'm sorry." Hunter was asleep. "Hunter, I love you." Faith glanced at the clock—4:30 AM.

Words

Carla presented Hunter with miniature boats, adrift in a water-filled basin on the table. Preoccupied with his ability to open and close the dollhouse door, Hunter did not bother to look at Carla. Faith observed from Carla's desk.

Jack had a leash in his hand. Bow and Millie, small dogs, tugged at Hunter's heels.

Carla flicked water at Hunter's hand, asking, "Hunter, where's Hunter? Come over here, come over here, we can play with water, we can play with water come and see, come and see."

Hunter opened and closed the dollhouse door. Carla placed the water basin beside Hunter. He flung himself into Jack's lap, and the dogs jumped at Hunter with tongues out, ready to kiss.

Faith insisted, "Jack, the kids need to go outside."

Carla received wet kisses from the dogs and asked, "Will Hunter play with the dogs?"

Jack guided the dogs out as he answered Carla, "He loves dogs. Right? Hunter loves dogs?" He gave Hunter a tap on the head.

Faith stepped from behind the desk. "The dogs would like to play in that water."

Jack hurried Bow and Millie out. Hunter trailed Millie but Faith caught him and guided him to the chair next to Carla. She placed his hands in the basin of water. Carla enveloped Hunter's hand in hers, picked up a boat off the table, and placed the boat in the water. Carla smiled, "Hunter's boat floats. Good job, Hunter. Good boy." Hunter stimmed, and the boats bobbed to the other side of the basin.

Jack re-entered and asked, "May I join you at the river?"

Carla winked, "Sure, Hunter, Jack plays." Hunter flicked a boat with his finger, abruptly shoved the table away, and climbed into Jack's lap. He stimmed.

Carla sang, "Give me a sailboat, give me sailboat." Hunter slid off Jack's lap, placed Carla's hand on the sailboat, and returned to Jack's lap.

The dogs sniffed under the door. Hunter slid off Jack's lap again, crawled over to the door, placed his nose under the door, sniffed, then laughed. Carla gleefully exclaimed, "Excellent interaction! Good boy, Hunter!"

As Faith and Jack reached for Hunter, their heads bumped. Carla laughed.

Jack rubbed his head and sat back down. "Ouch! You've got a hard head."

Faith turned Hunter around to face Carla. "So do you. Carla, when you get his attention I'll slip out the door."

"Okay, Faith. Hunter, look boat float, look—boat float."

Hunter stimmed, Jack cleared his throat and said, "Hunter, boat, look boat float."

Hunter stuck his hand in Jack's mouth. Faith slipped into the hall and tended to Bow and Millie.

Carla placed an Oreo cookie on the table. Hunter leaped up and snatched the cookie. He separated the top from the cream, licked the cream, and dropped the cookie on the floor.

Social Security Office

Faith spun quarters on the waiting room floor to keep Hunter occupied. One quarter escaped, rolled, and landed under the water fountain. Hunter followed the quarter and placed Faith's finger on the water fountain button. Faith pushed, released, and repeated, "Water on, water off, water on, water off."

"Hunter, Mommy has to use the bathroom, come." Faith slipped and grabbed the fountain to catch her balance. Hunter placed her hand again on the button, stared at the spout, and stimmed. "Please, little love, Mama has to go, there's water in the bathroom." Faith darted into the bathroom and turned on the faucet.

Hunter stopped at the doorway then he bolted to the other end of the waiting room and made himself comfortable near an old lady. She glanced at Hunter and smiled.

Faith rushed over and exhorted, "Hunter, this way, please, climb chairs, Hunter." Faith held Hunter's hand as he stomped, one chair at a time. Faith moved ahead to clear the path with polite commands, "I'm sorry, could you move, thanks."

Malicious comments filled the air: "That's not how you should raise a child!" "Does he do this at home?" "Bad parenting!"

Back at the bathroom, a security guard approached and said sternly, "Excuse me, lady, we have to sit on those chairs. It's not a gym."

Faith responded, "Sir, he's practicing for the Statute of Liberty run."

The security guard rolled his eyes. "Lady, please."

Faith pleaded, "Sir, is it at all possible for you to watch him while I run to the ladies' room?"

"No," the guard hurled at her as he returned to his post down the hall.

Faith hugged Hunter, lifted him from the chair, placed his feet on the floor, held his hand, dug in her bag for the Oreo cookies, unwrapped the package with her teeth, and used them to lure Hunter.

He stopped at the water fountain. Faith flicked water on his face, opened another Oreo cookie, and stepped into the ladies room. Hunter hesitated at the entrance. She snatched Hunter, rushed him into the bathroom. He grabbed on to the door jamb and held tight. Faith pulled back his fingers, unhooked his grip, and yanked him into the bathroom. Hunter kicked the door and howled a high-pitched scream. Faith locked the door, unzipped her pants, sat on the toilet and heard, "Security to the ladies room."

Seconds later, a security guard banged on the door, "Open this door immediately! Open up."

Hunter kicked and screamed louder.

Faith hollered out, "Sorry! My son despises bathrooms. One moment please. I can't believe this Hunter Shhhhhhhhhhhh!" Hunter continued to bellow and kick the door.

Faith grabbed the toilet tissue, zipped her pants, and flicked water from the sink on Hunter's face.

The guard banged on the door, "Open up!"

Faith responded harshly, "*Wait* please." She flung herself at the door, to block, in case the guard tried to open it. "Hunter, please stand up for Mommy." She flicked more water on Hunter's face, succeeding for a moment in making eye contact. Hunter stood.

The security guard kicked open the door. Faith gripped Hunter's hand and walked calmly past the security guard. "Sorry about that, my son hates bathrooms, sorry."

The guard questioned, "Miss, is that your child?"

Faith hugged Hunter closer to herself to protect him. "Yes, sir. We're here to get him evaluated by the social worker."

The security guard shifted his stance and said authoritatively, "Show me some ID."

Faith rolled her eyes and slipped her bag off her shoulder. "Sure, just a moment." She searched her bag. Oreos and pretzels dropped to the floor.

The guard shook his head in disbelief. "The way he sounded, his screams, it sounded as if he was being hurt."

Faith continued to search for her ID in her bag. She commented, "He will be a loud rock star." Faith handed over her drivers license along with a picture.

The security guard took the documents, read the license, and smiled at the picture. Faith fake giggled, "My friend thought that it would be cute to have a picture of Hunter pulling my hair."

The guard handed the items back, "Sorry, I just have to be sure."

Faith rearranged all the stuff that had fallen from her bag, "I understand, Hunter's a loud one."

The security guard touched Hunter's head gently. Hunter twisted his arm around, checked out his wrist watch, and stimmed. Faith explained, "He likes to watch the minute hand."

The guard smiled, "He's a handsome fellow." The guard shook Hunter's hand and returned to his post in the hall.

Over the speaker came a summons, "Faith Parker, please follow me."

The receptionist waited. Faith held Hunter and rushed down the hall. She speed- walked behind the receptionist through faded gray hallways into a dimly lit room. In the corner, behind a dilapidated desk, sat an elderly woman. Her clothes were as faded as the walls, her face was round, her hair in a messy ponytail. Her oversized sweater had holes in the elbows.

She welcomed Hunter with open arms, "Hello, young man, hello."

Faith lowered Hunter onto the desk. He crawled to the end, climbed up to the sooty window that overlooked the alley.

The receptionist slammed the door closed. "Please come in. Sorry you had to wait so long. My name is Helen Fall. I'm the psychologist."

Faith leaned on the desk. "Nice to meet you. This little caveman is

Hunter, and he is a little over two years old. Do you mind if I change his diaper real quick?"

"No, not at all, I'll just run out for my messages." Helen exited quickly.

Faith wrapped the diaper in a plastic bag and tied the bag in a knot. Hunter explored under the desk and around the dusty closet.

Helen hurried to her chair behind her desk. She said, "You can throw that out in the bathroom next door, thanks." Then, Helen suggested, "Let him roam. When you get back, I have to ask you a few questions."

Faith slipped out the door, returned in seconds, and sat in the guest chair.

Helen cleared her throat. "Faith, are you a single mother?"

"Yes."

Hunter was on the window sill. Faith placed him back on the floor.

Helen read from a sheet of paper. "Does the father see the child?"

Faith replied, "No."

Helen sneezed, opened her drawer, and pulled out a tissue, "Has anyone taught you how to manage Hunter?"

Faith cleared her throat, "No, not yet."

Helen said (in a low whisper), "Hunter, Hunter, come sit here with me."

Hunter climbed onto the window sill. Faith reached to retrieve him.

Helen placed her hand on Faith's shoulder to stop her. Helen whispered, "Hunter, Hunter, come sit here with me."

Hunter crawled closer to Helen and touched her arm.

Faith watched in awe.

Helen opened a picture book and held up the pictures for Hunter to see. Hunter crept closer. Helen continued to whisper, "Hunter, can you tell me what this is?" Hunter inched closer, until, finally, he was next to Helen. "Which one is the dog?"

Hunter stimmed, rocked, then pointed to the dog.

In soft tones, Helen continued, "Very good boy. Which one is the ice cream cone?"

Hunter pointed to the ice cream, then returned to the window sill.

Faith clapped her hands. "I am impressed. Should I whisper all the time?"

Helen shoved the book back into the desk drawer. "When he goes to school, the teachers should coach you. Don't use too many words, one or two words at most."

Faith retrieved Hunter from the window, "This is it?"

Helen smiled, "Yes, that is all, have a good day." Helen blew her nose into another tissue.

Hunter touched her arm, and Faith guided him out the office door. "Thank you again, Helen, I've learned already."

Helen smiled, "Could you tell reception to send in the next person?" Faith nodded and shut the door quickly.

Board Dogs

DOGS SNIFFED AROUND FAITH'S feet as she changed Hunter on the bench.

North bowled for the dogs. "Faith, I've lined a few dogs up for this weekend."

Faith tossed the diaper in the trash. "Yeah, sure. The last job of just watching two dogs turned into six dogs. North, at least tell the truth. I don't mind caring for them."

North babbled, "Okay, okay, the business is expanding, I have more for you to watch. You'll be fine. I've kept all these dogs at my palace before."

Faith watched Hunter with a close eye as he chased Millie around. "Are you on vacation?"

Two dogs lunged at each other. North stepped between them. "Just a break. You're my best employee."

Faith smiled, "My apartment's too small to board all those dogs."

North back-kicked the ball and pleaded, "Think of the money you will make this weekend. Get the roommate to help you watch the dogs."

Faith smiled, "You're a lazy ass!"

North cracked a smile. "Come on, Faith! Ka-ching ka-ching!"

Faith dodged for Hunter just before he stomped on a dog's paw. "The names of the weekend boarders please."

North reached into his pocket. "I have composed a list for you, the contact numbers, the types of food."

"Composed. That's a big word for you!"

North smirked and handed over the list.

She read it over. "Everybody eats the same. Do these dogs know each other?" Faith read the names, "Tenant, Irving, Bear, we love Bear, Silver-boy, Chardonnay"

North interrupted, "Don't steal my customers and start your own company while I'm away."

Faith whispered into North's ear, "Please! One week will be enough for me. Don't stay longer than that."

North inched away, "Stay ten feet back."

Faith laughed, "Are you sure you are visiting your mother and not an old girl? You are only going an hour away?"

North hurled the ball across the dog park and snapped, "Two hours."

Faith rolled the ball. "Okay, two hours. You could do that in a night. People do that every day, they're called commuters."

North laughed, annoyed, "Don't panic. The dogs are friendly, you have my mother's telephone number. Make sure it is an emergency."

Faith checked her watch. Hunter fell. "You are the boss." Faith scooted to Hunter.

North leashed his posse, tied them near the exit, and raised Hunter onto his shoulders. "How's the roommate, Jack?"

Faith leashed the dogs and responded suspiciously, "Fine. Why?"

North smirked, "I saw him in a restaurant with some girl. They were having dinner. Just so you know."

Disappointed, Faith closed the gate.

Eye Doctor

HUNTER DARTED BETWEEN ROWS of injured patients. Faith tugged on his shoulder. He dropped to the ground and wailed. Jack tapped Faith on the shoulder. Surprised, Faith asked, "Where did you come from?"

Hunter crawled over to Jack, and Jack knelt on the floor next to Hunter. Jack said, "Hunter, we have to stand together."

Hunter touched Jack's hand, and they lay together, quietly, on the floor. Several moments passed, then Hunter jumped up and tugged at Jack's hand.

Jack rose. "Give me five, good boy. No cry. No cry."

Faith gratefully tapped Jack on the shoulder, saying, "You're a life saver." Jack smiled at them both as Hunter crawled under a corner chair. Faith whispered, "Hunter, please roll out, roll out," Hunter turned his face away from Faith. "Please, Hunter, stand up."

Jack lay down on the floor, and Hunter inched out from under the chair. He tugged at Jack's hand to get Jack to stand. Jack snatched Hunter into his arms.

A nurse stepped out of the doctor's office and announced, "Faith and Hunter, please, room two."

Jack stood with Hunter on his shoulders and followed Faith to room two. Jack stopped at the door. "Faith, I have to meet a friend. I'll see you later."

Faith opened the bottle of bubble mixture she had in her bag and blew some bubbles for Hunter. The spin of the ceiling fan caught his attention, and he stimmed. Faith replied thankfully, "Thanks, Jack."

Jack kissed Faith on the head gently. She leaned on his chest and sighed.

The doctor entered the room with a warm welcome. "Hello, Faith, I'm Dr. Ling." Dr. Ling nodded hello to Jack as Jack slipped past and exited.

Faith took charge. "I'm Faith and this is Hunter." Dr. Ling smiled. Faith hugged Hunter on her lap and warned, "Dr. Ling, Hunter isn't very cooperative."

Dr. Ling knelt to reach Hunter's eye level. Hunter turned away. Dr. Ling said, "Hello, Hunter, pleased to meet you." Dr. Ling extended his hand to Hunter for a handshake.

Faith informed him, "Dr. Ling, he doesn't talk yet." Hunter wriggled away from Faith and dashed for the door.

"Faith, please hold him in your lap."

Faith scooped up Hunter. "Okay."

Hunter turned his head left to right, making it impossible for Dr. Ling to examine his eyes. Dr. Ling left the room and returned with a nurse. Together, Faith and the nurse held Hunter's head still. Hunter bellowed as Faith reassuringly repeated, "Please, Hunter, be still. Mama loves you."

Hunter squirmed out of Faith's grasp and rolled across the floor like a ball. Dr. Ling and the nurse watched as Faith picked him up. Once again, she held Hunter firmly in her lap, and the nurse held Hunter's head still.

"Quick, Dr. Ling, be quick, check to see, please," Faith implored.

Dr. Ling and the nurse knelt at Faith's feet, and the doctor held Hunter's eyelid open. He flashed the small light into the right eye, then into the left eye. Dr. Ling said, "Faith, that will be enough, his eyes are fine."

The nurse opened a drawer filled with lollipops and asked, "Would a lollipop help?"

Faith offered Hunter the lollipop. Hunter stormed out of the room. Faith took the lollipop. "That will help me, thanks. Wait! Hunter, let's go out together." Faith joined Hunter at the elevator bank. He stimmed, watching the doors open and close.

Dog Run, Late Afternoon

HUNTER RODE ON NORTH'S shoulders as North herded his hounds. Faith gathered the stragglers. North ordered in a nasty tone, "Get control of the dogs, Faith, your son needs you."

Over her shoulder, Faith shouted, "Of course, no problem. Look Hunter, Mama can't catch the dog." Hunter stimmed.

"Faith, you need to do something more important than chase the dogs right now."

Faith yelled, "One second! Here, Daisy, come here. *Now!*" Faith leashed Daisy and tied her to the fence.

North shouted again, "Faith, this is more important."

Faith rushed after Cash. The dog bolted to the opposite side of the park. She yelled over her shoulder, "One second, just got to get Cash. Cash, get over here now! Come, Cash, come get the ball, good boy." Faith yanked Cash's leash.

North barked tersely, "Faith, did you bring your bag for Hunter?"

Faith brought the dogs to North. She answered, "Yes I did. Tenant has it in his mouth."

Tenant's tail wagged. He was ready for play. North lowered himself onto the bench, slipped Hunter off his shoulders, and placed him on the bench.

Faith begged, "Tenant, don't move. *Please.*" Tenant, with her bag in his mouth, shook his head fiercely. Faith lunged for him and missed.

North still held the wailing Hunter on the bench. "Faith, come on, we have to get these dogs back. Hurry up."

Faith arrived beside them. "That dog loves this hot weather, always wants to play." North frowned. Faith asked, "What makes you so testy today?"

North hurried after Tenant. "I'll do it." North touched the handle of Faith's bag. Tenant bolted away.

Faith laughed, "It's not so easy, is it?"

North pulled a dog biscuit from his pocket. "The right props ... speak with authority. He knows what he can get away with ..."

Faith sniffed. "phew! Now I know, Mr. Hunter, phew. North, hurry with that bag!"

North moved to the center of the park and motioned for Tenant to come. Tenant shrank to the ground and crawled toward North. Faith commented, "That's mean, North. You are being mean to Tenant."

North checked his watch, irritated. "Check the time, Faith. We are late getting these dogs back."

Faith picked up her bag from the ground and kissed Hunter. "We need a new diaper. Smelly boy."

As Faith changed Hunter, North checked his watch again. "I have to get to the bank before it closes."

Faith dressed Hunter. "Would you get me a money order for the rent? I have the cash." Cash ran over and pounced on Faith's legs. "No, not you, Cash, good boy." Faith threw out the dirty diaper and wiped her hands with a Handi Wipe. She retrieved an envelope from her bag and handed it off to North. "Since you're doing that, I'll take Tenant and Cash, plus my usual dogs, home."

North counted the money and commented, "There is two thousand dollars in here."

Faith laughed, "You can count! Good boy."

North was concerned. "You behind on the rent?"

Faith replied, "Yes, so get four money orders at five hundred a clip."

North smiled at the cash. "Will do."

"Well, didn't that money put a smile on your face? Feel better?"

North stopped his count and smiled. "Feel great."

Faith leashed Tenant and Cash. "Don't steal it. Remember it's my rent money."

North smirked, "No, never." North anxiously gathered the dogs and offered, "Faith, I'll get you a bank check and drop it off at your rental office for you."

Faith belted Hunter into his stroller. "Do I detect an act of kindness?"

North smiled sweetly. "Helping a good friend. I'll do it tomorrow."

Faith was delighted. "That would be so helpful, thanks. Home beasts."

As Faith walked out of the park, a stroller wheel got jammed in a pothole. North glanced back as she shook the stroller hard to free the wheel. The dogs barked. Faith yelled over the barking dogs, "Hang on, Hunter!" Faith ran, and Hunter held Tenant's leash; the hounds trotted alongside them.

Speech Therapy

HUNTER PROUDLY SAT ON Jack's lap on the floor, squinting his eyes at the breeze from the high speed fan. Carla held a plastic brush and firmly rubbed Hunter's arm up to the shoulder, then down to the wrist. The exercise got her a big smile from Hunter. Carla repeated the arm rub several times. Faith said, astonished, "That's amazing. He's so relaxed."

Carla explained, "This is very good sensory stimulation. Watch how I very gently go up, then down between the elbow and wrist on the inside of the arm. Hunter is happy." Carla handed the brush to Jack and commanded, "Please rub his arm the way I did, Jack."

Jack rubbed Hunter's arm. Hunter rested his head on Jack's chest and closed his eyes. Carla suggested, "Faith, would you like to try?"

Faith shook her head. "Not now, but I'll buy the brush—where can I pick up one?"

Hunter bolted for the dollhouse. Carla stopped him, and Jack moved the dollhouse to the table. Jack commented, "He loves that game. He opens and shuts the doors in the apartment a lot." As Hunter played, Jack narrated, "Hunter, door open, door close." Hunter tried to push him out of the chair and Jack laughed.

Carla sat beside Hunter and displayed tiny animals in front of a barn. She pointed to a cow. "Hunter, a cow says *moooooooooo*." Carla touched the cow's head; the cow released a loud *moo*. Carla tapped the bee, causing a loud buzz. "Hunter, a bee says *buzzzz*."

Carla passed Jack a balloon. He held the balloon but it popped causing Hunter to jump. "Sorry, I broke his concentration." Jack said.

Carla checked her watch and stood up from the table. "Also mine. Perhaps it is too late in the day for Hunter."

Faith stood and commented, "We did have a big day today. Can we schedule for morning next week?"

Carla opened her calendar and replied, "Whatever is good for you, Faith. Hunter, we must put back the toys we have, the toys we have."

Jack and Faith helped Carla and Hunter put the toys back into the box. Faith leaned over to kiss Hunter. "Hunter, come, give me hands."

Hunter climbed into his stroller and screamed. Carla spoke over the yelling, "Faith, I can fit you in next week at 9:00 AM."

Faith shouted, "That'll be fabulous."

Carla slipped out from behind her desk with a CD. "Music is very important. Try this Mozart CD, and let me know how Hunter responds."

Faith examined CD jacket. "I actually have a Mozart CD. I'll give it a try. Thanks." Faith made sure she had a firm hold on Hunter's hand before they exited into the bright sunlight. Hunter covered his eyes with his shirt. "My goodness, Hunter, we need to get you sunglasses."

Hunter pulled his shirt over his face to cover his eyes. Jack gave Hunter a kiss, and Faith tilted her head close to Jack for her kiss. Jack withdrew, annoyed. "I have to go. I'll meet you back at the apartment." Jack held open the door.

"Jack, you'd better give us a head start. I don't want him to see you leave." Faith rolled the stroller down the block looked back, Jack walked across the street and hailed a cab. "Hmm, I can't figure him out." Hunter dragged his feet. Faith stopped. "Is something wrong?" Hunter pointed to the giant ice-cream cone in front of a store. Faith smiled, "I guess you don't need to talk." Faith released the stroller seatbelt, and Hunter tipped over the stroller as he climbed out. "Jeez, Hunter, be careful." They entered the ice cream store.

Jack's Exit

FAITH PEERED AT THE three large men who were squeezed into a small car that was parked along the curb near her stoop. Faith got up from the stoop to enter her building. Hunter held onto the banister with white knuckles and screamed, kicked, and lay on the ground, kicking the sidewalk. A passer-by muttered, "Give that kid a crack on the ass. Spoiled brat."

Faith ignored the comment and cooed, "Hunter, Mama loves you, we can come back out later." Faith began to sing, "Time for inside, time for inside, time for inside the house."

Frank sauntered down the block and stopped in front of Faith. "You can hear him scream from the avenue. Hunter, what is the matter? Is your mother beating you?" Frank swished his long keychain by Hunter's eyes. Hunter reached out for the chain, his screams halted.

"Thank God you showed up. Where were you, the park?" Faith removed a juice bottle from the stroller. "How about some juice, little man?" Hunter snatched the bottle.

Frank posed. "Yes, I laid out in the park all day. How's my tan?"

Faith poked his arm. "Wow, extreme tan! Are you using sunscreen?"

Frank twirled and caught a glimpse of the large men in the small car. He remarked excitedly, "Faith, did you call for a sex service?"

They watched the men line up outside the car. The tall, thin, nondescript man leaned on the car; the second man had a medium frame with an extended beer belly; the third man was short and stocky with an authoritative look.

"No, I did not. I think they're cops."

The beer-bellied man used his cell. The nosy neighbor arrived, passed the men, gave Faith and Hunter an evil look, and entered the building. The men rushed past Faith, Hunter, and Frank. They entered on the neighbor's tail.

Frank surmised, "Those men are probably after your roommate."

Faith rolled her eyes. "You just don't like him. He's been very supportive with Hunter, came with us to therapy, pays the rent promptly."

Frank snapped back, "It's only been six weeks."

Faith insisted, "Hunter, time to go inside. Hunter, are you ready?" Hunter swung the keychain over his head. Frank snatched it back as Faith took Hunter's hand. "Yes, we are ready." Faith lobbed her bag over her shoulder, Hunter reached out, stopped the bag mid-swing, retrieved the water bottle, and tossed the bottle to the sidewalk. Faith reached out but missed the bottle. It crashed to the ground. "Oh hell!" The bottle rolled into the gutter. "Hunter, that's a *No*. Please, Frank, get that bottle before it rolls further down the street." Frank stepped off the stoop and scooped the bottle off the ground.

Just then, the three misshapen men emerged from the building with Jack. Jack's hands were cuffed behind his back. The tall, skinny detective opened the car door; the beer-bellied detective hopped behind the wheel; and the authoritative detective escorted Jack to the backseat.

Faith, startled, asked, "Jack, what happened?"

As Jack was shoved into the car by a detective, the detective commanded, "Don't say a word."

Frank questioned, "Should we hold the apartment for you or are you relocating?"

Jack shouted from the backseat, "Definitely hold the apartment, thanks. Don't worry, Faith. I'm sorry."

The authoritative detective joined Jack in the backseat and slammed the door. The beer-bellied driver started the car as he slammed his door, Faith and Frank watched the car merge into traffic on the avenue.

Frank noted, "Roommate down. Quick, get upstairs, let's see if he has any money hidden in his bags."

Frank led the way. Faith advised, "We have to have respect for his space."

Frank had his key ready to open the door. "I didn't say throw them out, just go through them."

Faith peeked over at Hunter from Jack's room. Hunter stimmed in front of the television. Frank sat in the middle of six large garbage bags. As he examined each item, he threw it into a 'checked' pile.

Frank busily turned out the pockets of Jack's jeans. "What does this tell us about Jack?"

Faith flung a sweater into the pile. "So far, I find that he prefers sweatpants to jeans. He has crazy geometric T-shirts, and he saves all of his receipts."

"Excuse me, Faith, I found a collection of ladies' telephone numbers."

Faith sneered, "Why would he save those numbers?"

Frank replied sarcastically, "Not sure. Maybe he runs an obscure prostitution ring."

Faith defended Jack. "That's not enough of a lead. Wonder what he's charged with?"

Frank opened a garbage bag and spread out the cash receipts. "He can afford to eat out a lot."

"He never asked me." Faith opened a box and gasped, "I need a drink!"

Frank slid on his butt over to the box, opened it slowly, and gasped, "Look at the bundles of money."

Both touched the cash. Faith slapped Frank's hand. "Be careful," she warned. "He probably knows exactly how much."

Frank grabbed a bundle. "Let's go to dinner!"

Faith countered, "Can we order in?"

Frank flipped through the bundles. "There must be at least thirty thousand dollars!"

Faith knelt near the money. "I could pay off my charges." She slammed the lid on the box. "All that money and he uses garbage bags. Amazing."

Hunter ran into the room, climbed on the pile of clothes, then ran out to the kitchen and screamed.

Faith hurried after Hunter. "Frank, do you think he'll call?"

Frank threw his arms up in the air, placed them on his hips, and glared at Faith. "Jack will be back like a bad dream."

Hunter howled in the kitchen, and Faith kissed him. "Hunter, you okay?" She shouted to Frank, "Frank, throw everything back in the bag. Frank, before you leave that room, grab a couple of fifties."

Frank placed all the garbage bags over the clothes and shut the door. He stuffed a fifty-dollar bill in his pocket and gave one to Faith.

Frank Takes Charge

THE DOGS HELD GREEN balls in their mouths and watched Frank roll Hunter through the gate. They dropped their balls at Frank's feet. "Get back, you hounds!" he shouted.

Hunter struggled to escape and gave a strong kick toward Frank's head. Frank dodged the foot and said uncertainly, "Faith, I don't know about this."

Faith sighed and hurried over to the stroller. "No kick, Hunter, no kick. Faith kissed Hunter's feet and pleaded, "Please, Frank. Hunter's a bit restless. Please, just for a few hours. The bus leaves at 3:00 PM, and, after a couple of hours on the bus, I have to get a cab to the prison."

Frank stood and stepped back from the stroller. "You made the guest list?"

Faith searched in her purse for bubbles and passed them to Frank. She gazed up at the sky. "I can only hope."

Frank inquired, "Does North know your past lovers?"

Faith folded a blanket from the stroller, "No, and do not tell him. North is a good guy, remember, he went to the bank for me."

Frank sashayed over to Faith. "You do him yet?"

Faith covered Hunter's ears. "Could you be quiet? He will hear you. No, the answer is no."

Frank patted the dogs before he chucked the ball. "Oh, does he prefer the dogs?"

Hunter kicked the stroller with his feet and pointed. Faith handed a folded piece of paper to Frank. "Frank, here is a list of Hunter's favorite words, take it."

Frank stuffed the list in his pocket. "The kid can't talk, and you have a list of favorite words."

Hunter began a very low hum that gradually developed into a wail. Faith knelt down and kissed Hunter. He pulled her hair. She untangled the strands of hair from Hunter's clenched fist and backed away from him. "Ma loves you, baby." Frank rolled his eyes. "Frank, it's time," she added.

"Yes, I can see that Hunter wants to go."

Faith snapped, "So go."

Frank huffed, "Okay!"

Faith cheered, "Hunter, Hunter, look! Aunt Franka's taking you to the park. P a r k, say it, repeat after me. P a r k." Hunter focused on the ground, and Faith lovingly kissed him again. "Be nice, Hunter, give Mama a kiss." Faith kissed Hunter again on the head.

The dogs surrounded Hunter and Faith and licked their faces. Frank pushed the dogs away. "Ewwwww. We are off to the p a r k. Call when you get back from the penitentiary. See, there's always a reason why men don't call." Frank waved, adding, "Faith, tell Stone I would love to be on that guest list to service all his needs."

Faith smiled, "I will relay the message. Bye, bye, good boy, be good for Aunt Franka."

Frank pushed the stroller into a pothole. "Get out and walk, kid!"

Faith replied, "Make sure it's not in traffic."

Frank pulled the stroller free and walked briskly toward the park. "Tell the father to take Hunter and return him when he is twenty."

North wrapped the dog leashes in one hand and helped Frank move the stroller onto the sidewalk. Frank checked out North's butt. "Hey, North, I see you have a new dog. What's the fellow's name?"

North glanced over at Faith, then answered, "Red." North approached Faith and shrugged his shoulders. She watched Frank push the stroller toward the park. North asked, "Is Frank good with kids?"

Faith pet Red. "Hunter loves his Aunt Franka." She shouted, "Aunt Franka, make sure he drinks lots of water. It's hot."

Aunt Franka responded using a gesture with his middle finger.

North cleared his throat and adopted a serious tone. "Faith, I need a favor. This weekend, I need you to keep about a dozen dogs overnight. Just one night."

Faith got angry. "Are you nuts? I cannot help you with a dozen! Sure to be evicted."

North touched Faith's hand gently, slipped her a hundred-dollar bill.

Faith glared at North and snatched the hundred. "You must be desperate. How much will I get for caring for the dirty dozen dogs?" North smiled, "Do this for me, and I'll let you keep all the money, just this once."

"Visiting your mother again?" Bear nudged Faith for attention. Faith pitched the ball, North kicked a few balls; the beasts were busy.

"No, running an errand for a good friend."

Faith shot back, "Always so secretive. Is it one of the pet owners?" Bear brought the ball back, and Faith pitched it again.

"Why do you think that? No, it's not one of the pet owners."

Faith laughed, "My theory is—Bear's always with us all day, I thought you had something going on with his owner."

North slid the ball from Bear's mouth and hurled it. "Bear's owner is a man; I am not into men, if you don't mind."

Faith shook her head. "Bear's owner is a woman. I met her when I walked Bear the first day you hired me. Are we talking about the same dog called Bear?"

North chewed on his fingernails. "Oh, yeah, that's right." As he darted to the other side of the dog run, a bag of pot fell from his pocket.

Faith plucked the bag off the ground and held it up for North. "Before you go away mad, you might want this."

North turned, reached over Tenant, grabbed the bag, and stuffed it back into his pocket. "What time you getting that bus?"

Faith herded the dogs, "So, that's what's bothering you? The bus trip? He's my son's father."

North opened the gate and tugged at his group's leashes. "That's not what's bothering me. Can you help me out with the dogs?"

Faith gathered her dogs. "Don't be so grouchy. Be nice."

North checked his watch. "I am nice."

Faith touched North's hand, surprising him with the touch. "Most of the people in my building will be away, so, yes I'll do it, but this is the last time, North."

Gleefully, North exclaimed, "I'll never fire you, you know that" You are my best worker."

Faith guided her dogs. "I'm your only employee. What are you really talking about?"

The dogs began a slow trot. Faith held their leashes tightly as they all walked down the street together. North turned left at the corner, Faith turned right.

The Visit

FAITH SHOVED HER BAG into a locker at the main entrance. A guard checked a list; another guard escorted Faith across the yard to a secured area.

Faith got her hand stamped at the window. The stamp was immediately checked under ultraviolet light. The guard proceeded to walk Faith and others to the main visitors building. Faith listened to the guard's instructions: "After your visit is finished, cross the yellow line that's on the floor, and wait for a guard to escort you out of the visitors building."

The guests paraded to the gloomy building.

Faith leaned on the wall opposite the prisoners' entrance. Stone was escorted into the hall. She smiled, recalling why she had fallen for him. His shoulders were wide, his arms were strong, and his hair was thick. She spoke to herself, "Jeez, all my men look alike, I'm nuts, crazy for Mr. Wrong."

Stone approached, in his oversized orange jumpsuit, with a wide grin. The guard released the cuffs from Stone's wrists.

Stone waved and greeted her, "Hi." He remained near Faith in awkward silence.

Faith waved back and responded, "Hi, nice outfit."

Stone bantered back, "It comes with the room."

Faith shot back, "Always good to see a man in uniform." She looked around the big room. "Lots of people."

Stone smiled, "All criminals."

Faith nodded in agreement. Stone chewed on his fingernails and stared at the floor. Faith huffed.

After an awkward pause, Stone broke the silence. "How did you find me?"

Faith smiled, "Internet. Thanks for leaving my name at the door."

Stone leaned into Faith for a brief hug. "Why did you come? Something wrong?"

Faith retreated a few feet back from Stone. "Something wrong? What gave you that idea?" She swung into an orange chair.

Stone copied her, sitting one seat apart. "We broke up long before I booked my room, and you're here."

Faith dropped her head into her hands and sighed, "Since you asked."

Stone leaned forward in his chair. "Oh shit."

Faith sighed heavily and glanced at Stone. "Would you like the short story or all the details? It concerns your child, Hunter."

Stone, confused, asked, "Who's Hunter?"

Faith turned away from Stone and murmured, "Your son. I know I told you it was a girl but in actuality, you have a son."

Stone exclaimed joyfully, "You lied! I have a son." He lunged at Faith and gave her a bear hug. She continued to babble, "You were AWOL when you thought it was a girl."

Stone held Faith. "The girl would be yours; a son is mine."

Faith broke the hold. "Custody is not why I'm here."

Stone, delighted, plopped down in the chair. "Why are you here?"

Faith focused on the tiled floor. "When is your lease up?"

Stone rose and began to pace. "Three years. Why did you lie about the child?"

Faith pointed to the chair for Stone, he followed the command and sat. Faith continued, "Um you were misinformed, that's all. At the time you were running around, drugging, sexing. I would not want my child involved with any of that chaos."

Stone bolted out of the chair. "That's how we met. You're no angel. Remember the night we met, we stayed in bed for days"

Faith gazed around the room. "Let's see, only angels stay in this establishment."

A guard passed by, and Stone returned to the chair. "Did you bring any pictures?"

Faith spit out, "You know you can't bring anything in here. I'll have to mail them. Hunter looks like me."

Stone thought for a moment. "Why did you choose the name 'Hunter'?"

Faith sat straight and took Stone's hand in hers. "To me, the name 'Hunter' symbolizes strength."

Stone said, "Weird name. Bring him to visit me."

Faith leaned in closer and whispered, "Are you nuts? He has a disability."

Stone released her hand and shouted, "What?"

Faith's fierce look silenced Stone. "Hunter falls in the autism spectrum. He has been seen by a psychiatrist, and he's in speech therapy—stuff like that."

Stone fidgeted in his chair, then leaped up and paced in front of Faith. "Therapy? He is two years old! Give him a chance. Some kids talk late. I didn't talk until I was three years old."

Faith stuck out her foot. Stone tripped and glared at her. She asked, "Do you remember if you responded to commands, like 'get your shoes,' or 'turn the light on'?"

Stone took a seat across from Faith. "You're crazy. No, I don't remember. The quacks are running a scam on you."

Faith, frustrated, continued. "I am helping my son get better. To think—I sat on a bus for three hours to see your ass."

Stone blurted, "It takes an hour and a half to get here. Who you kidding?"

Faith stormed across the yellow line. Stone stopped at the yellow border. Faith kept her back to Stone and said, "Still a rude mother fucker."

Stone sighed, "Please, I'm sorry, Faith. I'm sorry. Please."

Faith didn't budge. The guard came over to escort out the visitors who had gathered.

Stone continued, "Please, Faith, I'm not good at apologizing. Please."

A second guard entered with new visitors. Faith's jaw dropped, and she raised her hand to her mouth to muffle her gasp. The nosy neighbor had entered on the left with the new group.

Faith grabbed Stone's shoulder. "Ouch!" Stone yelled, relieved. "Faith, what's going on?"

Faith whispered, "Do you remember my annoying neighbor? She kept knocking at the door and demanding that we turn down the music?"

Stone sighed, "Yeah, why?"

Faith answered, "She's in here." Stone scanned the room for her. Faith poked him. "Don't do that. I'm sure she already saw me."

Stone recollected, "That night was so crazy. She kept banging on the wall and yelling, 'turn down the music.'"

Faith nodded. "I thought for sure she would call the police. I remember, I tripped over your shoes and slammed my head on the wall so hard I saw stars."

Stone laughed, "You could hear your head crack. She was so mad she banged on the door and buzzed that buzzer. You answered, your head cut, blood dripping all over your face, and she screamed, then you screamed."

Faith laughed, "You came out smoking a joint, naked, and she ran back to her apartment. What a night!"

Faith got a warm hug from Stone, and she smiled. She moved toward the snack area. "Starving."

Faith slid a dollar bill from her pocket and slipped the bill into the machine. The machine spat the bill back out, and it floated to the floor. Stone picked the dollar up and inserted the bill into the machine. The machine accepted the bill.

Stone whispered, "Go ahead Faith, it's your dollar."

"Hmm. These are Hunter's favorite cookies." Faith opened the wrapper of the Oreos and passed one to Stone.

He took her hand and held it gently. "Thanks, Faith. I appreciate you showing up. Could you send some pictures? I'd like to have some pictures."

Faith fired back, "Stone, that'll cost you."

Stone offered, "I make twelve cents an hour." Stone energetically swung into a chair beside Faith.

Faith twisted the Oreo top off the cream. "You have any Ben Franklins buried?"

Stone kissed her hand. "Sorry. No treasure."

Faith rolled her eyes. Stone ate one cookie and took another Oreo out of her hand. Faith grabbed the cookie back, "Hey, I gave you one."

Stone pulled Faith close to him, engulfed her in his arms, and gave her a passionate kiss. The guard's voice came over the speaker, "Take it easy."

Stone released Faith, and she caught her breath. "Hmm, well, hmm, that was unforgettable."

Stone leaned back, satisfied. "Payment for the pictures."

Faith handed him a third Oreo. Stone twisted the cookie top off to eat the icing first. Faith brushed crumbs from his chin. "Hunter eats it that way."

The Swing

HUNTER FLEW HIGH ON the swing. Frank's monologue continued, "Hunter, Hunter, say 'higher, higher.'"

Impatient nannies complained, "That man (they pointed at Frank's back) has had his son on the swing for a long time. Teach your son to share."

Frank ignored the comment and continued to push Hunter. "Hunter, say 'A, B, C, D, E, F, Geeee.'"

An older nanny protested, "That child has been on that swing for far too long. Give someone else a chance."

A younger nanny joined the taunt, "Don't make my child cry, you're a rude person. You have to teach your children right."

Frank didn't respond to the rebellion but continued talking to Hunter. "Hunter, what do the wheels on the bus do? That's right, they go round and round."

A nanny aggressively slid beside Frank. He slipped away and pushed Hunter from behind. The elder nanny pointed her finger at him and warned, "Sharing is an important quality that must be taught to a child. Your mother didn't teach you did she?"

Frank ignored them and focused on Hunter, pushing him higher.

The younger nanny said, "Time for lunch, let's go, time for lunch."

Frank repeated, "Time for lunch."

The rebel elder retrieved her stroller, grabbed a bottle, and handed it to her crying child. The younger Nanny led the way out of the swing area, commenting, "He won't be there later. Come, we'll feed the children and come back."

Frank watched them relocate to the benches before saying, "Hunter, I thought they would never leave, please get off the swing now while they're busy." Frank stopped the swing and lifted Hunter. Hunter kicked and screamed. Frank readjusted Hunter in the swing and pushed the swing higher. Hunter laughed. Frank kept up the song, "A for apple, b for ball, c for cat, and that's not all."

A petite, curly–red-haired au pair, armed with a baby, tapped Frank on the shoulder. "Sir, I don't mean to be rude but that child has been on the swing for twenty-five minutes. The swing is for all the children in the park."

Frank kept the swing high, blurted out a verse, "B is for bottle, I is for ink, T is for tolerance, C is for cat, H is for house."

The au pair's mouth dropped open. She placed her hand on her hip and said, "You spelled 'bitch.' He's spelling bitch to his child."

Those that waited for the swing gave Frank the evil eye.

Hunter screamed and raised his hands in the air. Frank maneuvered Hunter out of the baby seat. Hunter's shoe caught on the strap of the swing so Frank slipped Hunter's shoe off and lifted Hunter straight up above his head until Hunter's feet were free. Frank held Hunter in his arms and dragged the stroller to a safe zone outside the swing section. Hunter insisted on walking so Frank held Hunter's hand when they cross the street.

In middle of the avenue Hunter dropped, screamed, and kicked. Frank retrieved Hunter, and Hunter slammed Frank's stomach with his foot. Out of breath, Frank yelled, "Hunter, this is not the time for this. Please get up *up*! Hunter, *up*. I'll leave you here in the middle of the road." Frank walked two feet away, and Hunter crawled in the opposite direction. Frank reached for Hunter. "Hunter, no, this way. This way."

Frank opened his arms and lunged, scooping Hunter from the ground. He dashed back to the corner, dragged the stroller behind him, and anchored Hunter between himself and the wall of the park. He searched his pockets for the list. Hunter tried to wiggle free and screamed. Frank spoke over the hellish screams. "Where's that list your crazy mother gave me? It has your magic words on it. Do you remember any of your magic words? Hunter, I'm talking to you. Stop! Stop screaming and answer me!" Frank yanked the list out of his pants pocket, " Never mind, I got the list."

Frank held Hunter securely on the ledge of the park wall, and, with his free hand, unfolded the list. Hunter continued to bellow and kick. Frank fought for control. He held Hunter at eye level and read the words. Hunter slipped in slow motion to the ground and lay on the sidewalk. Frank knelt beside Hunter and stared into Hunter's eyes. Hunter squeezed them shut. Frank read, "Okay, Hunter, love, say l o v e, chips, Hunter likes ***chips***! How about, ***bus, truck, telephone, numbers***, was your mother drunk writing this list? Where oh where's a ***balloon***?" Frank struggled with Hunter, and Hunter yanked his hair. "Ooooh, you ***brat***." Frank shouted, "Hunter, you are a *challenge*."

Hunter laughed at the sound of the word *challenge*. Frank slowly repeated, "***C h a l l e n g e***, challenge, challenge, c h a l l e n g e, weee." Hunter lay very still, only for a moment, then bolted to his feet. Frank grabbed Hunter's hand with a strong grasp, and they peacefully walked across the street. Frank kissed Hunter's hand and said, "Your mother has her hands full with you."

Hearing Test

A THICK GLASS WINDOW PANE divided the young intern with the controls from the floor where standing speakers were affixed to each side of the small room. A toy monkey with cymbals sat on top of the left speaker; the right speaker held an elephant with cymbals. A child's chair was in the center of the room, and scattered stuffed animals made the room friendly. A pair of headphones hung behind the chair.

Hunter flipped over a box of marbles, and escaped marbles rolled freely around the floor. As Faith hurried to collect them, the intern entered. She handed him the forms.

He glanced at Faith's notes and asked, "Why is he here?"

Faith answered sternly, "My son, I'm told, is in the autistic spectrum. I'm here to make sure he's not deaf."

The intern responded, "Okay, I'll give him the basic test."

The intern reached for the headphones and slipped them over Hunter's ears. Hunter ripped them off his head and tossed them to the floor. The intern again adjusted the headphones on Hunter's head; again Hunter discarded them to the floor.

Faith suggested, "Can we do this without the headphones?"

Frustrated, the intern wrapped the earphone wire tight around the earpiece. He replied, "We can send the sound through speakers, but it's not very efficient."

Faith suggested, "Please, let's try that. He doesn't want to wear them."

The intern exited and reappeared in front of the window. He dimmed the lights, then slowly sent extremely low sounds through the speakers, switching between the left and right sides. Hunter turned his head in the correct direction each time.

The intern dimmed the lights further, making the monkey barely visible. The intern caused the monkey to tap its cymbals. Hunter, spooked, leaped into Faith's lap.

Faith laughed, "Hunter, love, look—a monkey. Look monkey." Faith sniffed, kissed Hunter's head, and snickered, "Excuse me, sir," She tapped on the glass divider. "You scared the shit out of him. Time out, please."

The intern responded with a smile, "The test is over. Please return to the waiting room for the results."

The Puddle

FAITH STRETCHED OUT HER arm from under her umbrella to check for rain drops. "Okay, guys, this is your last walk for the night." She flung the ball, and dogs pushed, nipped, and pounced on each other trying to retrieve it first.

Hunter loved the rain on his face. He stimmed and watched the dogs play. Tenant returned the ball, and Faith placed the ball in Hunter's hand. Bear snatched the ball from Hunter, and Hunter laughed. Faith kicked the ball, the dogs chased after it, and Hunter ran with them. Faith noticed a gigantic puddle along the route home and said to herself, "I hope Hunter did not see that—he'll go right for it."

"Time to go home before rain gets worse. Let's go," Faith called out as she leashed the dogs one by one, placed Hunter under her arm, and guided the dogs through the exit gates.

Hunter slipped from Faith's grasp and ran toward the puddle. Faith called, "Hunter, do not go that way! This way! This way, my love." Hunter ran faster toward the puddle. Faith led the pack and chased Hunter, shouting to the dogs, "Guys, I knew it. Oh hell."

Faith dropped the leashes. The dogs barked at the edge of the puddle as Hunter laughed and splashed. Faith ordered, "Don't sit down! Hunter, no sit, no sit." Faith gathered the dogs and hooked them to the fence. She barked at them, "Don't move a muscle, I'll be right back. Everybody, sit."

Faith waded into the water, cooing at Hunter, "Come, my love, bath time, come on, love. ***P l e a s e***."

Hunter splashed knee-deep in the puddle and laughed. Faith trailed along, repeating, "Hunter, fun, fun, love, we must go home, clean water at home, come on, Hunter."

A jogger ran past the puddle and blurted, "Slap that kid on the ass. He'll listen."

Faith dropped her shoulders and yelled, "Shut up! I'll sic my dogs on you."

Faith caught Hunter's arm and swooped him into her arms. She dashed out of the puddle. Hunter screamed, bucked, pulled Faith's hair, and stabbed his chin in her chest. "Hunter, the water is a ***no***. Ready, one, two three, weee." Faith swung Hunter in the air, in a half spin. She secured him under her arm, held him like a football, collected the dogs, and rushed toward the exit. She muttered, "Don't trip me, you hounds, don't trip me. Wait, Wait, break."

Faith stopped and caught her breath. Hunter was anchored on the ground between Faith and the fence. Once Hunter was unable to move, she rearranged the leashes. Hunter howled, screamed, and kicked.

A woman approached Faith and asked, "You need some help?"

Faith looked up. "Sure, can you hold these?" Faith handed her a few leashes but the woman lunged at Hunter.

"This is how you take care of this."

Faith threw out a punch, hitting the woman's shoulder. "Excuse me, don't touch my son."

The woman seized Hunter's jacket. Faith yanked the jacket out of her grasp. The woman defiantly stared at Hunter. "Stop crying right now, young man," she commanded.

Faith shoved the woman away and wrapped Hunter in her arms. The woman held her ground, stared unafraid.

Faith was infuriated. "Step away, woman, step away," she said. Faith turned Hunter away from the woman and pulled the dogs closer.

The retreating woman shouted, "That child should be on medication."

Faith responded, "Medication is what you need, lady! Take a double dose of valium! Bitch!"

The woman hurried to cross the street.

Hunter repeated, "Bitch."

Faith excitedly kissed Hunter and exclaimed, "Your first word! Good boy." Bear nudged Faith, and she placed Hunter on his back. Hunter laughed and held on to Bear's collar. Faith gathered other leashes, still holding Hunter. Tenant slipped away from the group. Faith halted his escape by stomping on Tenant's leash. Faith yanked on the all leashes, shouting "Break time!" The dogs surrounded Hunter and showered him with kisses.

The Nerve

FRANK INHALED AND COUGHED, "Smells like wet fur in here. Disgusting."

Faith slapped chicken nuggets on a plate and shoved the plate in the microwave. Dogs sniffed for crumbs on the floor. Faith tugged the shade up and said sharply, "Look, it's raining. Fur gets wet, smells!"

Frank smiled and read the eviction notice on the table. "Give it to me straight. What happened?"

Faith grabbed Hunter's stimming hands. She said, "Stop that please." Spitting out her words efficiently, she answered, "North obviously did not get the money orders for the rent; he's off somewhere spending my rent money."

Frank peered at her over the document. "Is he in Atlantic City?"

Faith snarled, "There was not enough cash to get him to Vegas."

Frank asked sarcastically, "Has he called?"

Faith hurled back, "Do men ever call? That's a stupid question."

The microwave rang. "Faith, there's the bell for round one. This is his business. Let all the dogs out to fend for themselves." Frank opened the door and shooed the dogs. "Get out, dogs. Go dogs, get out of here!" Tenant licked Frank's feet, Bear sniffed around the door jamb, and Cash woofed, cueing the others to join. Frank laughed at Faith's annoyed look.

She shouted over the noise, "What are you doing?"

Frank demanded, "Get out, dogs! You'll see how fast you can ruin North's life."

The nosy neighbor climbed the stairs. She frowned and held her bag close to her body, away from the dogs. She dropped her keys then quickly stomped her foot over them to prevent the beasts from sniffing them.

Faith apologized, "Sorry, sorry."

The neighbor glared wickedly at Faith as Faith herded the dogs back into the apartment and slammed the door. "I quit, I quit after this walk."

Frank returned to the table. Hunter climbed on his lap.

Faith yanked open drawers and slammed them shut. "Where's my résumé?"

Frank laughed, and Hunter wiggled free. He threw his nuggets on the floor and returned to his position in front of the television. The dogs fought over the nugget pieces.

Faith wrenched a piece of paper from under a pile of books. "Here it is!"

Frank cheered, "Faith, go and walk these beasts."

Hunter was comfortable in his rocker, sipping his juice. Faith kissed him on the head. "Hunter, I'll be right back."

Frank nudged Faith in the butt with his foot. She fell on the floor, "Get out with the beasts," he said. "Do you have enough paper?"

Bear kissed her as she leashed him. "Buzz me in, bully." Faith stood and gathered the leashes.

Frank urged, "Hurry up."

The bell on the microwave rang. Frank was exasperated; Hunter laughed at the animation and stimmed. Frank flung open the microwave door and waved the smoke around. "I told your mother I can't cook." He wrapped the one good nugget in a napkin and passed it to Hunter, then he threw the rest out. Hunter stimmed, the smoke rose to the ceiling.

Help

FAITH PAUSED AT THE church door, gathered the leashed dogs, opened the heavy door, and guided her dogs through main entrance. She whispered, "You guys wait out here, I'll just be a minute," as she tied the leashes to the back alter gate.

Faith blessed herself with the holy water and slipped into the last row. She peeked back at her dogs. They were peaceful. She knelt down to pray and placed her face into her hands. She heard a bellow from the alter and peered through her fingers. She huffed, spying her neighbor. Faith waved. The neighbor slammed the kneeler, stomped out of the pew, quickly stormed by Faith, kicked by the dogs, and shouted, "*Sinner.*"

Bear whispered, "Woof," and tugged at the knot with his teeth. Tenant yanked until the knot released. They crept in quietly. Bear leaped to sit next to Faith. Both dogs were respectfully silent. Faith peeked to her right, smiled at her crew, and continued to pray.

Suddenly, Tenant's ears shot forward. He pointed his tail back, froze, and poised for attack. Bear growled and barked. Faith sighed, gathered the dogs, and ran out. Tenant scampered out last, dragging his leash behind. Faith stepped on Tenant's leash, scooped it up, and ran with the dogs down the street, brushing away tears.

"Oh miss, excuse me, miss!" Frank called out.

Faith laughed, "Are you cruising with my son?" Faith yanked the leashes. The dogs sat. Hunter pulled Tenant's ear and grabbed at the leashes. Faith kissed Hunter's hand, and he pulled away.

Frank continued, "I can't believe you were in there with all those smelly beasts, in God's house."

"We are all God's children!"

"Give me some of those leashes."

Faith obliged. Frank made the sign of the cross, then took Hunter's hand and did the same. "Thank God the walls didn't come tumbling down. We're all good." Bear led the pack across the street.

The Psychologist's Office

HUNTER GAZED AT, BUT did not touch, the puzzle in front of him. He spotted a silver truck on the floor, shoved himself away from the table, and plucked the truck from the floor. He flipped it over and spun the wheels. The psychologist watched.

Hunter abruptly dropped the truck, opened the dollhouse door, and closed it. He then opened and closed the door many, many times.

The psychologist jotted notes as he spoke to Faith. "You will receive my report in the mail. Hunter will need a lot of one-on-one attention to help him."

Faith watched Hunter open and shut the dollhouse door. She asked, "Do you have any openings at this school?"

The psychologist filed papers in a folder. "Yes, we do for the fall. I'll make sure the application is enclosed with our report. Hunter's older, we are starting a bit late with him."

Faith hung her head and sighed. "Late? Some say their children did not speak until three or four years."

The psychologist gathered papers into his notebook and led them to the door. "Faith, you are on the right path now, we have very good teachers who will work with Hunter to improve his interaction and communication skills."

Faith reached for Hunter's hand and said appreciatively, "Thanks, thanks very much." Faith kissed Hunter on the head, and he pushed her away and continued to open and close the dollhouse door. Faith covered the dollhouse door with her hands. "Hey, caveman, come." She swooped Hunter into her arms, and the psychologist smiled. Hunter attempted to push her away, battling her a mighty grip. The psychologist held the door open for Faith, and she rushed Hunter out. The psychologist politely closed the door.

The Money, Returned

FAITH ROLLED HUNTER DOWN the street, and he dragged his feet on the ground. They halted in front of the bus stop. Hunter stimmed as he watched people unload from the bus and other people get on the bus. The driver waved for Faith to board. She called, "No, driver, we are not traveling. We like to watch."

North sneaked up to the bus stop. Faith allowed the dogs to lick Hunter's face. North patted Hunter's head, and Faith immediately jerked the stroller away. Hunter slammed his feet on the wheels, stopping the stroller.

North feebly apologized, "Faith, I'm sorry."

Faith crouched down, readjusted Hunter's feet, and grabbed the keychain from the stroller basket. She slapped the keys into North's hand and demanded, "Show me the money, North. show me the money."

North held his team tightly and fired back, "You made a lot last weekend, dog sitting."

Faith stood with her hands on her hips and delivered her lines in a nasty tone. "You stole two months rent. Shall I march right over to the police station?"

North pulled an envelope from his back pocket. "Okay, here, the exact amount."

Faith opened the envelope, fanned the hundred-dollar bills, and counted out two thousand dollars. "Where's the interest?"

North tugged on leashes and the dogs sat. "Come on, Faith. That's exactly what I used. Sorry."

Faith placed the money in her bag and walked away from North. He caught up again with a request, "Can you walk some dogs for me today?"

Faith spat back at him, "No! I told you I quit. No more."

The hounds barked for Faith's attention, and Hunter laughed. Faith smiled sweetly at her son and touched his cheek.

North tossed out, "The dogs love you."

Faith pet the dogs and moved on without looking back. She shouted words into the hot air, "North, it was fun but it is over now. Good bye."

North watched Faith hurry away, and his last words followed faintly, "Faith, you need a reference, call me."

Faith responded, "You did not make the résumé cut." Faith rolled the stroller across the street, and North redirected the dogs in the opposite direction.

Interviewed

LIZ, THE OFFICE MANAGER, peered at Faith over the résumé. "You have a very good résumé. Please, explain the gaps."

Faith cleared her throat. "During my time at Ericson Ericson Fan's, I fell in love and took time off to have my son. On maternity leave EEF's merger finalized and my attorneys left the firm. My time at Freeze Gill Lark was brief because I became aware of my son's autism. It was necessary for me to take time off to spend more time with him. Presently all is well and I'm ready to work here at Robert Gold Larolson's."

Liz smiled, "Well done. Are you prepared for the spelling, writing, typing, and word tests? It should take about two hours. The tests are done in another office. Follow me please, and I'll get you set up."

Faith slung her bag over her shoulder. "Great."

Liz prepared the computer for the tests with several clicks on the keyboard. Faith placed her bag in the empty chair.

Liz stood at attention and delivered the instructions, "Please type in your name in the box. Hit enter, then the test will begin in sequential order. If you have time afterward, I would like you to meet the attorney."

Faith responded, "Sure." Faith pulled the chair close to the desk and keyed in her name. Liz stepped out of the office and closed the door.

Faith walked through the streets to her next appointment. She checked her watch, entered a tall building, showed ID to the security guard, and received a pass. She stood at the elevator bank and waited.

Cathy, the office manager, met Faith at the reception area. Faith followed her to the office. She reviewed Faith's résumé and yawned. "Faith, give me an example of your best and worst quality?"

Faith thought for a moment, then responded, "My best quality, punctuality, got to be to work on time. An example of the worst, mmmmm, worst, I'd have to say not taking a lunch."

Cathy answered with annoyance, "That's not really an example I was looking for. Let me ask you this. What came first, the chicken or the egg?"

Faith thought for a moment. "Was there a rooster involved?"

Cathy placed the résumé down on the desk, "Are you ready for the spelling, writing, typing, and word tests? It should take about two hours."

Faith inhaled energetically. "Ready."

Cathy led Faith out the office. "We have to go to another office. Follow me please, and I'll set you up."

Faith slung her bag over her shoulder followed, "Great."

Cathy clicked the mouse to retrieve the program. Faith placed her bag in an empty chair. Cathy ordered, "Type your name in the box and hit enter. The tests will begin in sequential order. If you have time afterward, I would like you to meet the attorney."

Faith pulled the chair close to the keyboard. "Sure." Faith adjusted the chair, Cathy exited the office. Faith closed her eyes and muttered, "Oh, Jesus, help me get through this day. These tests suck." Faith clicked the keys for the timed typing test.

Sitter Frank

KIDS SCOOTED DANGEROUSLY CLOSE to Hunter as he focused on the drain in the main artery of the park. Hunter pointed to the letters, and Frank spoke slowly, "Hunter, d r a i n. D r a i n. This is a drain."

Bus brakes squealed, and Hunter ran parallel with the bus to his lookout bench. He stimmed as people got on and off the bus.

Frank informed Hunter, "That's right, Hunter, people off, off the bus, and on the bus."

Hunter jumped to the next bench and landed near an old lady who was reading. Hunter's stimming motions annoyed the elder, and she relocated to another bench. Hunter leaped into Frank's arms. Frank caught Hunter, wobbled forward, caught his balance, hugged Hunter, and swung him over to the nearest picnic table, placing Hunter's feet on the table top.

Hunter stomped over the table top, and Frank laughed, "Mr. Hunter's very heavy. Jump to the ground, Hunter. You can do it."

The old lady slammed her novel shut, and said, angrily, "You should teach your child manners. Does he stand on the table at home? Very bad manners."

Frank fired back, "Excuse me, I do not understand your point. Are you making a point?"

The old lady used her book like weapon, waving it at Frank's face, "Are you the father?"

Frank dodged the book and sassed, "Uncle, cry uncle."

The lady tucked her novel into her sack and stormed away.

Hunter leaped into Frank's arms. Frank balanced Hunter's weight, moved backward to the table, and sat down. "Hunter is heavy," he repeated. Hunter poked Frank in the eye. Frank took Hunter's hand and said sharply, "No!" Hunter laughed. "I'm going to tell your mother you're a brat." Frank bear hugged Hunter and wiped his eye with his shirt. Hunter watched attentively and stimmed as another bus unloaded. Frank tickled Hunter's back and Hunter protested with a scream.

Frank screamed louder, "Pizza! Pizza!" Hunter ran to the opposite side of the park with Frank in hot pursuit. Frank chased him through the sprinkler. At the sandbox, Frank shouted, "Don't roll in the sand, Hunter." Hunter rolled from one end of the sand to the other, Frank shrugged his shoulders, checked his watch, "Hunter, are you hungry would you like pizza? P i z z a. Yum, yum p i z z a."

Hunter lifted his head in the direction of the bus stop as one pulled up to the curb. He scurried to the park bench and stimmed; people exited and boarded the bus.

Frank held Hunter in his arms and pointed Hunter's arm in the direction of the Pizza restaurant, "Pizza place please." Hunter bolted toward the exit. Frank grabbed Hunter's shirt, guided him through the sprinkler, rinsed off the sand, retrieved their towel from the fence, and wrapped the towel around Hunter.

Pizza

FRANK COMMANDED, "STAY HERE, please." He pushed Hunter's chair tight against the table. Frank moved Hunter's face to direct his attention to the ceiling fan, "Watch." Frank proceeded to the counter; Hunter pushed out his chair, moved to the table under the clock, and stimmed.

The pizza maker called out, "Kid, watch." Hunter stimmed, under the clock. The pizza maker clapped his hands together loudly. Hunter turned to face the pizza maker and watched him toss the dough, spin it, catch it, and slap it on the counter. The pizza maker sprinkled the dough with flour. Hunter stimmed.

Faith entered and gave Hunter a big hug and kiss. "Hunter, my love, how are you? Frank, order me a slice please." She continued, "My love, are you watching the pizza fly?" Hunter grabbed Faith's hand and led her directly to the door. Faith bear hugged Hunter and gave him a kiss. Hunter pushed her away.

Frank commented, "See, he wants you to leave."

Faith was surprised. "I just got here, Caveman, I want some pizza. Frank, do you have some money to cover for me, babe."

Frank smirked and paid for the order. "I'm not made of money, bitch."

Hunter wiggled out of Faith's grasp and returned to his chair. Frank served pizza. Faith peeled the cheese off of Hunter's slice.

Frank dabbed his napkin on his slice. "So, how did it go?"

Faith sprinkled garlic salt on her slice. "Test, test, test. I'm sure I got some bore ass job. 'Mr. Tell's office. He's at a meeting, would you like his voicemail?'"

Frank folded his pizza in half and raised it to his mouth. He asked, "Did you hear from the school?"

Faith dabbed Hunter's mouth with a napkin, and Hunter pushed her hand away. "I have the letter here." Faith retrieved the envelope from her bag and placed it on the table.

Frank pushed the envelope to Faith. "Read it, bitch, don't keep us in suspense."

Faith opened the letter and read, "Hunter has been accepted to the learning center, oh, a name tag." Faith peeled the name tag seal off, placed the tag on Hunter's shirt. Hunter ripped it off and flung it on the floor.

Frank snickered, "That's the spirit, Hunter. Don't do anything she tells you."

Faith continued, "Hunter, you get to take the school bus. Oh boy. We have to get you up at 6:00 AM to catch the bus at 7:00 AM."

Hunter left the table, and Frank leaped to fetch him. Faith gathered their belongings and ordered, "Get him, Frank."

Frank spit out, "Don't tell me what to do, Missy. I've been fetching him all day." Frank clutched Hunter's hand, "Come on, Hunter." Frank and Hunter proceeded to the corner, ten paces ahead of Faith.

The Return of Jack

Faith and Frank held Hunter's hands tightly as they walked down the street toward home. Frank gasped, "He's out already!"

Faith glanced at Frank. "Who?"

Frank glared at Faith. "Your roommate."

Jack relaxed beside two garbage bags on the top step of the stoop.

Frank tapped one bag with his foot. "Where do you buy your luggage?"

Jack grinned. "This is my waterproof line. Hunter, how's my little man?" Hunter snuggled on Jack's lap and handed him a package of Oreo cookies. Jack complied, opening the pack and handing a cookie to Hunter.

Faith smiled lovingly. "Jack, you trusted us with some of your treasure, not to mention a number of bags. Shall I get them?"

Jack leaned over and gave Faith a kiss on the cheek. "The treasure, my treasure, it's still in the box?"

Faith smiled, "I borrowed a couple of months rent."

Frank stood back and folded his arms over his chest. "The rent has gone up, you are a high risk tenant."

Faith asked, "Are you headed for the slammer?"

Jack stood up and responded, "With respect for your time I'll be brief. I'll pay two hundred a week for that room."

Together Frank and Faith responded, "Where did you get the treasure?"

Jack stepped back and picked up Hunter. "I'm going to baby-sit Hunter while you're at work, no charge."

Frank's arms went into the air. "What, are you nuts?" Hunter kissed Jack's face, reached for Faith's hand, and placed it on Jack's hand.

Jack smiled, "Well, what do you think?"

Faith smiled at Hunter. "Hunter has offered his opinion."

Frank directed, "Take the offer. Give him a kiss to seal the deal Faith."

Jack returned Hunter's kiss, placed Hunter on his shoulders, stretched his arm around Faith, and squeezed her in a group hug. Jack called out, "I'll give you a hug after hours, Aunt Franka."

Frank rolled his eyes. "I'll be waiting for that hug."

Faith yanked the apartment keys from her bag. Hunter proudly balanced on Jack's shoulders, and Frank yelled, "I'll be over later."

As Faith inserted the key in the lock, the door was flung open. She dropped her keys as the neighbor shoved herself between Faith and Jack, paused, smiled seductively at Jack, and slammed the door.

Faith sneered, "Oh, she smiled at you, Jack. Do you know her?" Hunter belted out a scream that drew Jack and Faith back to the stoop. Jack lowered Hunter from his shoulders to Faith's open arms, "What's the matter?" Hunter slipped into Faith's arms, then slid down her body to the stairs. Hunter picked up a shiny quarter and held it in his hand.

Jack laughed, "He forgot his money."

Faith kissed Hunter. "Honey, let mommy have that. Not in the mouth, not for eating." Faith wrestled the quarter away from Hunter.

Jack held the door open and winked. "Let's get upstairs." He swooped Hunter back on his shoulders.

Faith slipped past Jack. "I have the keys, I go first."

Jack smiled, "What's for dinner?"

Faith climbed the stairs and suggested, "You can order in. We ate pizza."

Twilight Chat

FAITH BALANCED HER MUG of wine in one hand and used her foot to boot open the door. She glanced to her left and Frank high-kicked over to Faith, who was now seated on the stoop.

"I've been waiting for five minutes. So how's life with the man?" Frank asked.

Faith took her place on the top step, sipped from the mug, and smiled. "Both men are asleep."

Frank huffed, "Isn't that typical." Annoyed, he swung down beside her.

Faith covered her ears, and Frank gave her a quizzical look. Faith sassed, "Don't you hear the cement cracking?"

Frank returned fire, "Not my ass, your butt did the damage." Frank leaned back on the wall. "Well, how was the first day at work?"

Faith rolled her eyes. "Work is always the same—irritating. I met people there that I used to work with at EEF. Life won't be so bad, same hours 9:30 AM to 5:30 PM. Today I just filled out papers." As Frank covered his yawn, Faith tossed out, "Hey you asked."

Frank straightened up his posture, leaned into Faith, and whispered, "You can tell me, did you do him yet?"

Faith sipped from her mug and whispered seductively, "I ripped his shirt off, he carried me to bed, (she licked her lips) I still feel the pressure of the long hot kiss. I traced his firm chest with my tongue, climbed aboard his thick muscular thighs, and returned his passionate kiss."

Frank smacked Faith's arm. "You're a liar."

Faith laughed, "You're right. He ordered food from the deli, went out to meet someone, and came home late. When I was ready to go to work, I knocked on his door. He got up and sat beside Hunter at the television. Nobody said 'bye.' When I got home, Hunter was laughing, Jack had him in a plastic bin and he lowered and raised him like he was in an elevator." Faith smiled and sipped her wine. "Hunter was so happy, it made me smile."

Frank sashayed down the stairs. "I waited all day to hear something juicy."

Faith sipped her wine. "Jack decided that it would be best not to get involved. He doesn't want any trouble."

Frank shook his head. "He doesn't want any trouble and he's living with you."

"Frank, eventually, there will be trouble, give it some time. You should be proud of me, I have a man in my house." Faith jumped at noise from the loudspeaker. Frank marched to the loudspeaker and said, "Delivery."

Jack's voice came over the speaker. "Faith, Hunter's throwing up, and his nose is bleeding bad—hurry!"

Frank squished up his face. "Ewwww!"

Faith collected her mug and ordered, "Buzz me in!"

Frank swayed toward home, caught glimpse of a man on the corner, and sauntered down the street calling, "Oh, young man, young man, hello!" He disappeared around the corner.

Afterward

Dave worked on the apartment that Faith, Hunter, and Frank moved into together. Jack moved out with the treasure and was never heard from again. Stone was employed by Tight Leash and walks dogs for North. Lila returned to watch Hunter. On quiet mornings, you can still hear Hunter screaming.